Les took in Marla's hair as he followed her down the stairs.

Her hair fell straight on both sides of the part, and he liked the way it swayed as she walked. He noticed, with a start, that it looked like Mrs. Hargrove's coffee when it was being poured into one of the larger church mugs. Which, now that he thought about it, wasn't a half-bad piece of poetic nonsense for a rancher to come up with.

He silently thought the words, "Your hair is like coffee, pouring straight to—straight to…"

Well, Les told himself, he'd finish the words later. It was the thought that counted. Women liked poems about their hair. Byron, the poet, would never have found the words to an image like that, Les told himself with satisfaction. Maybe he'd put some sparkles in Marla's eyes yet.

Janet Tronstad grew up on her family's farm in central Montana and now lives in Turlock, California, where she is always at work on her next book. She has written more than thirty books, many of them set in the fictitious town of Dry Creek, Montana, where the men spend the winters gathered around the potbellied stove in the hardware store and the women make jelly in the fall.

Shepherds Abiding
in Dry Creek

Janet Tronstad

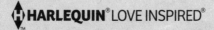

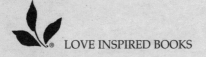

LOVE INSPIRED BOOKS

Recycling programs for this product may not exist in your area.

ISBN-13: 978-1-335-80700-7

Shepherds Abiding in Dry Creek

Copyright © 2007 by Janet Tronstad

All rights reserved. Except for use in any review, the reproduction or utilization of this work in whole or in part in any form by any electronic, mechanical or other means, now known or hereinafter invented, including xerography, photocopying and recording, or in any information storage or retrieval system, is forbidden without the written permission of the editorial office, Love Inspired Books, 195 Broadway, New York, NY 10007 U.S.A.

This is a work of fiction. Names, characters, places and incidents are either the product of the author's imagination or are used fictitiously, and any resemblance to actual persons, living or dead, business establishments, events or locales is entirely coincidental.

This edition published by arrangement with Love Inspired Books.

® and TM are trademarks of Love Inspired Books, used under license. Trademarks indicated with ® are registered in the United States Patent and Trademark Office, the Canadian Intellectual Property Office and in other countries.

www.Harlequin.com

Printed in U.S.A.

And there were in the same country
shepherds abiding in the field, keeping watch
over their flock by night.
—*Luke* 2:8

Dedicated to my grandfather, Harold Norris.
I remember him for his small kindnesses
and his big heart. He was a good man.

Chapter One

"I am the good shepherd; the good shepherd giveth his life for the sheep."

John 10:11

Marla Gossett sat in her bare apartment on the one wooden chair she had left to her name. The apartment building faced a busy street in south central Los Angeles, with the constant hum of cars going by. Marla didn't even hear the noise any longer. She'd sold her sofa yesterday and the kids' beds the day before that. She wished she could at least take the beds with them, but they wouldn't fit in the car when they moved. Besides, they all had sleeping bags.

Right now she was in the middle of selling her lamp to the African-American woman who had moved in down the hall a week ago.

Marla had given up on selling the chair she was sitting on. No one was willing to buy it with "XIX" carved into the arm. Not that she blamed them. She felt uneasy just sitting on the thing herself. She had put a notice in the hallway a week ago and several people had asked about the chair until they saw the numbers.

"You'll have a new life away from here," her African-American neighbor—Susan was her name—said softly. Susan was looking at these numbers on the chair. "Your son?"

Marla nodded. She wasn't proud that her eleven-year-old son, Sammy, had carved the sign of the 19th Street gang into her furniture. She told herself it was only natural for young boys to be impressed with the tough guys that ruled their neighborhood. The 19th Street gang was the largest Hispanic gang in Los Angeles. She knew her son was just an onlooker at this point. Other people didn't know that, though, and they were scared to buy the chair even if it was solid oak and had been the finest piece of furniture she owned.

The chair had been a wedding gift, and there was a matching wooden cross that came to hang behind it.

Susan looked up from the chair. "Well, I

guess they have gangs everywhere. Where are you going, anyway?"

"A place called Dry Creek, Montana. My husband had an uncle who left us a house there before he died."

"Did your husband get a chance to show it to you?"

Marla shook her head. She had already shared her vital statistics, so the woman knew her husband had died from lung cancer last year.

"Well, at least he left you with something," Susan said in a tone that implied she didn't expect much from men. "Of course, it would have been better if he'd gotten you some life insurance."

"We always thought there was plenty of time."

The woman nodded, and Marla wondered how it was that death had become so commonplace. Some days she wanted to scream at the injustice of it, but more often it just weighed her down with its ordinariness.

She had been a widow for over a year, and it still felt like yesterday. She'd married Jorge when she was nineteen, and it hadn't taken long for the blaze of romance between them to settle into a steady flame of affection. At least, she had assumed the flame was steady. That was the way it had been on her side.

The cancer came hard and swiftly. It wasn't until Jorge was gone that she had had time to think about her marriage. Near the end, when he could barely speak, Jorge confessed he'd been unfaithful several times and pleaded with her to forgive him. He said he didn't want to die with those sins on his conscience.

After his diagnosis, Jorge had started praying often and had asked her to move their wooden cross into the bedroom. It seemed to comfort him, and Marla was glad for that. She believed her husband did repent his sins. So what could she do? There was no time to work through her feelings. She forgave him because she had to, and then he lost consciousness, dying later that same night.

When he was gone, all Marla could think about was their marriage. She kept wondering if something was lacking in her, and if that was why Jorge had not loved her enough to be faithful or to even talk to her about his problems. Maybe she didn't inspire love the way other women did.

Even when he'd proposed, Jorge had not made any grand gestures of love toward her. Marla had not thought anything was wrong with that, though; she thought it was just the way he was. Marriage wasn't all about roses and valentines. She'd accepted that. But had she missed some clue? Or were there many little clues she had ignored? Was a woman supposed to keep a tally of things that would tell her if her husband still loved her? How could she not even have known he was unfaithful?

As her feelings for Jorge changed, Marla wondered if she'd ever really known her husband. Still, especially in the past few weeks, she'd wished he were still alive so they could share the problems about Sammy. Jorge might have been unfaithful to her, but he had loved Sammy. What would Sammy do without his dad?

Worrying about Sammy had made her take the cross out of the box, where she'd put it after Jorge died, and hang it on the wall again. Sometimes she'd look at it, searching for the solace her husband had found in it. She wished she could find an answer for Sammy there. The cross didn't speak to her the way it had to Jorge.

"Did you say Montana?" Susan was frowning for the first time.

Marla nodded. She wondered why the mention

of Montana was disturbing her neighbor more than their earlier discussion about death had.

"They don't have much color there."

"You mean trees?"

Susan pursed her lips as she turned to study Marla. "No, I mean people."

Marla had combed her hair this morning, as she did every morning. It was freshly washed and fell smoothly to her shoulders. At thirty-five, she knew she was no great beauty, but her skin was light olive, and she'd been told her eyes were nice. Her brown hair didn't sparkle with highlights, but she looked all right. She wondered why Susan was looking at her with such an intense expression.

Her neighbor finally nodded. "You'll do fine, though. I'd guess you're—what—half Hispanic?"

"On my mother's side."

Susan kept nodding. "And your son and daughter. I've seen them. They could be white."

Jorge had been half-and-half—Hispanic-Anglo—as well. That had been one of the things they had in common. "They pride themselves on being Hispanic, especially my son."

Susan grunted. "That's just gang talk. He'll get over it quick enough when he's away from here."

"I'm not sure I want him to get over it," Marla said stiffly. "He should be proud of his roots."

So much had been taken from them. She had to draw the line somewhere.

"Take my advice and blend in," Susan said as she picked up the lamp. "You've got a better chance of getting a new husband that way. Especially in a place like that."

"But—" Marla protested. She wasn't sure if she was protesting hiding her roots to find a husband or looking for a husband in the first place. She supposed she would have to marry if she wanted a new father for her children. But she wasn't ready for that yet. What if a second marriage proved only how lacking she was as a woman? There was no reason to believe she'd do any better the second time around than she had the first.

"Trust me. No one wants to have a Hispanic gang member in their neighborhood, no matter where they live. If they don't know you're Hispanic, there's no reason for them to make the 19th Street connection."

"But Sammy's not in the gang. Not really."

Susan held up her hands. "I'm just saying these people will be nervous. There was an article in *Time* magazine last month—or was it

Newsweek? Anyway, it was about gangs sending scouts out to small towns to see about setting up safe houses there. They want to have a place to send their guys so they can hide out from the police if things get bad. I wouldn't blame a small town for being careful."

"Well, of course they should be careful, but..."

Susan looked at the carving on the armchair again and then just shrugged. "I had a cousin drive through Montana a few years ago. If I remember right, he said the population is only about two percent Hispanic for the whole state. How big is this Dry Creek place you're moving to?"

"Two hundred people."

Susan nodded as she pulled the agreed-upon five-dollar bill from her pocket. "Then you and your kids will probably be the token two percent."

Marla frowned as she stood up. She was ready for the woman to leave. "We're probably not that far from a large city. Maybe Billings. There'll be all kinds of people there."

Susan snorted as she finished handing the bill to Marla. "All I can say is that you'll want to take your chili peppers with you. I doubt you'll find more than salt and pepper around there. It's beef and potato country in more ways than one."

Marla slipped the bill into her pocket. "We don't have a choice about going."

She didn't want to tell her neighbor that the police had come to her door a little over a week ago and warned her that Sammy was on the verge of becoming a real member of that 19th Street gang. She figured they were exaggerating, but she couldn't take a chance. She had given notice at her cashier job and started to make plans. She had to get Sammy out of here, even if it made every soul in Dry Creek nervous. At least she would own the house where they would live, so no one could force them to leave. Sammy and her four-year-old daughter, Becky, would be safe. That was all Marla cared about for now.

The neighbor took one more look at the scarred chair. "I guess we all do what we need to do in life. It's too bad. It was a nice chair."

Marla nodded.

"I wish you well," Susan said as she started walking to the door. "And, who knows, it might not be so bad. My cousin said they have rodeos in the summer and snow for Christmas. He liked the state."

Marla mumbled goodbye as the neighbor left

her apartment. She'd been anxious about the move before talking to Susan. Now she could barely face the thought of going to Dry Creek. But looking down at the arm of that wooden chair, she knew she had to go. She'd lost her husband; she refused to lose her son, too.

She wouldn't hide their ethnic roots from the people in Montana, but she saw no reason to advertise them, either. And, of course, she'd keep quiet about Sammy's brush with gang life, especially because it would all be in the past once she got him out of Los Angeles. She was sure of that. She had to be. Dry Creek was her last hope.

Chapter Two

A few weeks later

Les Wilkerson knew something was wrong when his phone rang at six o'clock in the morning. He'd just come in from doing the chores in the barn and was starting to pull his boots off so he wouldn't get the kitchen floor dirty while he cooked his breakfast. It was the timing of the call that had him worried. He'd given the people of Dry Creek permission to call him on sheriff business after six and it sounded as if someone had been waiting until that exact moment to make a call.

Les finished pulling off his boots and walked in his stocking feet to the phone. By that time, enough unanswered rings had gone by to discourage the most persistent telemarketers.

"I think we've had a theft," Linda, the young

woman who owned the Dry Creek café, said almost before Les got the phone to his ear. She was out of breath. "Or maybe it's one of those ecology protests. You know, the green people."

"Someone's protesting in Dry Creek?"

Dry Creek had more than its share of independent-minded people. Still, Les had never known any of them to do something like climb an endangered tree and refuse to come down, especially not in the dead of winter when there was fresh snow on the ground.

"I don't know. It's either that or a theft. You know the Nativity set the church women's group just got?"

"Of course."

Everyone knew the Nativity set. The women had collected soup-can labels for months and traded them like green stamps to get a life-size plastic Nativity set that lit up at night. Les was sure he'd eaten more tomato soup recently than he had in his entire life.

"Well, the shepherd's not there. We don't know what happened to him, but we can't see him. Charley says that Elmer has been upset about all of the electricity the church is using to light everything up. He says someone either took the shepherd or Elmer unplugged it to protest the whole thing."

Les had known there would be problems with people eating all that soup. It made old ranchers like Elmer and Charley irritable. It was probably bad for their blood pressure, too.

"Unplugging something is not much of a protest. It could even be a mistake." Now, that was a whole lot more likely than some high-minded protest, Les thought, and then he remembered promising the regular sheriff that he would be patient with everyone. "But I'll talk to Elmer, anyway, and explain how important the Nativity set is and what a sacrifice everyone made so we could have it."

Les was sure Elmer would agree about the sacrifice part. He'd said he was eating so much soup he might as well have false teeth.

There were some muffled voices in the background that Les couldn't make out over the phone.

"That's Elmer now. He just came in and he claims he didn't unplug anything. He says if we can't see the shepherd, it's because it's not there and Charley's right that somebody stole it."

"The light could be burned out." Patience went only so far, Les thought. He wasn't going to go chasing phantom criminals just because someone *thought* something was stolen. There hadn't been an attempted theft in Dry Creek since that woman had broken into the café two years ago. And she had not even taken anything. After all that time, it wasn't likely someone would suddenly decide to steal a plastic shepherd.

"Maybe it is a defective light," Linda agreed. "But I'm going to tell Charley and Elmer not to go over and check. It's still pitch-black outside. Charley's been looking out the café window for a good fifteen minutes, and it's still too dark to see if the shepherd is there. And if it's not there, then it could be a crime scene and we'd need the professionals." Linda's voice dipped so low that only Les could hear it. "Besides, the two of them could fall and break half their bones going over there in the dark. You know how that patch of street in front of the church is always so slippery when we've had snow. So I'll tell them you're going to handle it. Okay?"

"Sounds good," Les said. He'd rather safeguard old bones than chase after imaginary thieves any day. "I'll be right there."

Les usually made a morning trip into town, anyway, before he drove a load of hay out to the cattle he was wintering in the far pasture. The little town of Dry Creek wasn't much—a hardware store, a church, a café and a dozen or so houses—but the regular sheriff guarded the place as if it was Fort Knox, and Les, who was the town's only volunteer reserve deputy, had promised he'd do the same in the sheriff's absence.

Just thinking of the sheriff made Les shake his head. Who would figure that a man as shy as Sheriff Carl Wall would ever have a wedding, let alone a belated honeymoon to celebrate with a trip to Maui?

It was all Les could do not to be jealous. After all, he was as good-looking as Carl, or at least no worse looking. Les even owned his own ranch, as sweet a piece of earth as God ever created, and it was all paid for. Not every man could say that. He should be content. But for the past week every time he thought of Carl and that honeymoon trip of his, Les started to frown.

If Sheriff Carl Wall could get married, Les figured he should be married, too. He was almost forty years old and, although he enjoyed being single, a man could spend only so much time in his own company before, well, he got a little tired of it. Besides, it would be nice to have a woman's touch around the place. Les knew he could hire someone to do most of the cooking and cleaning. But it wouldn't be the same. A woman just naturally made a home around her, like a mother bird making her nest. A man's house wasn't a home without some nesting going on.

Of course, Les told himself as he pulled his pickup to a stop beside the café, the sheriff had gone a little overboard with it all. He had completely lost his dignity, the way he had moped around until Barbara Strong agreed to marry him. Les would never do that. He had already seen too many tortured love scenes in his life; he had no desire to play the lead in one himself.

His parents were the reason for his reluctance to marry. They had had many very public partings and equally dramatic reconciliations. Les never knew whether they were breaking up or getting back together. The two of them should have sold tickets to their lives. They certainly could have used some help with finances, given the salary his father earned in that shoe store in Miles City. Half their arguments were about money. The other half were about who didn't love whom enough.

His parents were both dead now, but Les had never understood how they could be the way they were. They were so very public about how they felt about everything, from love to taxes.

As a child Les had vowed to stay away from that kind of circus. It was embarrassing. Growing up, he never even made a fuss over his dog, because he didn't want anyone to think he was becoming like his parents.

No, Les thought as he stepped up on the café porch, if he was going to get married there would be no emotional public scenes. It would all be a nice sensible arrangement with a nice quiet woman. There was no reason for two people to make fools of themselves just because they wanted to get married, anyway.

"Oh, good. You're here." Linda's voice greeted Les as he opened the door.

The café floor was covered with alternating black and white squares of linoleum. Formica-topped tables sat in the middle of the large room, and a counter ran along one of its sides. The air smelled of freshly made coffee and fried bacon.

Elmer and Charley were sitting at the table closest to the door and they both looked up from their plates as Les stepped inside. They had flushed faces and excitement in their eyes.

"They already went over to the church," Linda whispered as she closed the door behind Les. "They snuck out when I was in the kitchen making their pancakes."

Les could tell the two men were primed to tell him something. It hadn't stopped them from eating their pancakes and bacon, though. All that was left on their plates was syrup. Les walked closer to them. Fortunately, no one had ever suggested people should have soup for breakfast, so that meal had always been safe.

"It's a crime," Elmer announced from where he sat. He had his elbows on the table and his cap sitting on the straight-backed chair next to him.

"We thought maybe you were right about the light just burning out," Charley explained as he pushed his chair back a little from the table. "We didn't want to bother anyone if that was all that happened, so we went over to take a look."

"Looks like a kidnapping to me," Elmer declared confidently, then paused to glance up at Les. "Is it a kidnapping if the kidnappee in question is plastic?"

"No," Les said. He didn't need to call upon his reserve deputy sheriff training to answer that question. "It's not even a theft if someone just moved the figure. That's probably what happened. Maybe the pastor decided the Nativity had too many figures on the left side and put the shepherd inside the church until he could set it up on the other side."

Les reminded himself to get these two men a new checkerboard for Christmas. A dog had chewed up their old cardboard one a month ago, and now, instead of sitting in the hardware store playing checkers, they just sat, either in the hardware store or in the café, and talked. Too much talking was giving them some pretty wild ideas. He couldn't think of one good reason anyone would steal a plastic shepherd, not even one that lit up like a big neon sign at night.

Charley shook his head. "Naw, that can't be it. All of the wise men are on the other side. The pastor wouldn't think there are too many figures on the left. Not even with the angel on the left—and she's a good-sized angel."

"Besides, we know it's not the pastor moving things around, because we found this," Elmer said as he thrust a piece of paper toward Les. "Wait until you see this."

Les's heart sank when he saw the sheet of paper. He had a feeling he knew what kind of note it was. It had a ragged edge where it had been torn from what was probably a school tablet. There must be a dozen school tablets in Dry Creek. The note was written in pencil, and he didn't even want to think about how many pencils there were around. Anyone could have written a note like this.

Les bent to read it.

Dear Church People,
    I took your dumb shepherd.
    If you want to see him again, leave a Suzy bake set on the back steps of your church. It needs to be the deluxe kind—the one with the cupcakes on the box.
P.S. Don't call the cops.
P.P.S. The angel wire is loose. She's going to fall if somebody doesn't do something.
XIX

Well, there was one good thing, Les told himself as he looked up from the paper. There weren't that many people in Dry Creek who would want a Suzy bake set. That narrowed down the field of suspects considerably. He assumed the XIX at the bottom was some reference to a biblical text on charity. Or maybe a promise to heap burning coals on someone who didn't do what they were told.

"So it looks like the shepherd is really gone," Les said, more to give himself time to think than because there seemed to be any question about that fact, at least.

Elmer nodded. "The angel is just standing there with her wings unfurled looking a little lost now that she's proclaiming all that good news to a couple of sheep. You don't see anything standing where that shepherd should be."

The door to the café opened briskly and an older woman stepped inside. She had a wool jacket wrapped around her shoulders and boots on her feet. Les thought she still had to be cold, though, in that gingham dress she was wearing. Cotton didn't do much to protect a person from a Montana winter chill.

"Mrs. Hargrove, you shouldn't be walking around these streets. They're slippery," Les said to the woman. The older people in Dry Creek just didn't seem to realize how hazardous it was outside after it snowed. And they'd lived here their whole lives, so if anyone should know, they should.

"Charley told me some little girl was in trouble." Mrs. Hargrove glared at Les as she unwound the scarf from around her neck and set down the bag she was carrying. "Something about kidnapping and theft. I hope you're not planning to arrest a little girl."

Les stepped over to help Mrs. Hargrove out

of her jacket. "Someone stole the shepherd from the Nativity set. I don't even know who did it yet. But if it is a little girl, she'll have to be dealt with just like anyone else."

Les turned to hang Mrs. Hargrove's jacket on the coatrack by the door.

"Well, a little girl wouldn't have done that," Mrs. Hargrove said as she smoothed down the long sleeves on her dress. "Mark my words."

"Little girls can get into just as much mischief as boys."

One thing Les had learned in his reserve deputy sheriff training was that a lawman shouldn't make assumptions based on stereotypes about people. There were all kinds of stories about mob men who loved their cats and sweet-looking grandmothers who robbed banks in their spare time.

"Still, I say no little girl took that shepherd," Mrs. Hargrove said as she walked over to a chair next to Charley and sat down. "If she couldn't get the angel unhooked, she'd take the baby Jesus. What would she want with a smelly old shepherd?"

Les frowned. "Just because a man works with animals and lives alone, it doesn't mean he smells bad."

Les had a few sheep on his ranch, but the

only full-time shepherd he knew was Mr.
Morales, who lived in the foothills of the Big
Sheep Mountains north of Dry Creek. Les
figured bachelor ranchers needed to stick together. Once in a while he invited Mr. Morales
down for breakfast. Les decided he needed to
do that again soon. Smelly, indeed!

"Well, no, of course not," Mrs. Hargrove
agreed and had the grace to blush slightly. "But
still, I can't see that a little girl would—"

"Whoever took the shepherd wants to trade
him for a Suzy bake set—the deluxe edition."
Les walked over and gave the note to Mrs.
Hargrove. "That sounds like a little girl to me.
You recognize the writing?"

Mrs. Hargrove taught Sunday school and she
knew all the kids in and around Dry Creek.
When she finished reading the note, she looked
up and shook her head. "I don't recognize it,
but whoever wrote the note probably tried to
disguise their writing, anyway."

Everyone was quiet for a minute.

"Are any of the classes in Sunday school
memorizing the nineteenth verse of some
book?"

Mrs. Hargrove shook her head. "Not that
I know of. They wouldn't write it that way,

anyway, would they? XIX? That's Roman numerals."

"I wonder about the Curtis twins," Elmer said as he reached for his cup of coffee. "I don't think they'd mess around with numbers, but they like cupcakes."

"They like to *eat* cupcakes. Those boys don't want to *bake* cupcakes," Linda said. "Besides, they're too busy with their new sleds to think up a scheme like this."

Les shrugged. "I don't know. Those boys live close to the church. I can't see any of the ranch kids coming into Dry Creek on a night like last night. For one thing, we would have seen tire tracks over by the church."

Les lifted his eyebrow in a question to Elmer and the man shook his head.

"Since there were no tracks, it means it had to be someone who was already in town last night." Les let his words sink in for everyone. Somebody in the center of Dry Creek had taken that shepherd. If there were no tracks, they couldn't blame it on a stranger passing through.

"Pastor Matthew won't like it if his sons stole the shepherd," Charley finally said, and then glanced over at Mrs. Hargrove. He must have seen the frown on her face. "Of course,

I don't believe it was the Curtis twins. Not for a minute. They don't even know about Roman numerals. They can barely add up regular numbers."

"Nobody added the numbers," Les muttered before Charley could get himself in a spin. "They just put them out there."

"Well, the only other kids in town are those two new kids." Elmer stared down at his cup. "And what would they want with a shepherd? They've never even been to church."

There was another moment's silence.

"They've never been anywhere," Charley finally said. "We've heard there are two new kids, but has anyone ever seen either of them?"

Everyone just looked at each other.

"Just because no one's seen them doesn't mean they're thieves," Mrs. Hargrove protested. "We need to have open minds here."

"Still, you have to admit it's peculiar," Elmer said after a moment's thought. "We've all seen the mother, but she must keep those kids inside. The only reason we know about the kids is because there are three names on their mailbox and we know the woman is a widow, so it has to be a woman and her two kids."

The mailbox had sprung up next to the driveway of the old house when the woman and her children moved into town. Les figured they had not realized that everyone in Dry Creek collected their mail at the counter in the hardware store, so no one had any need for an individual mailbox by their house. The mailman made just one stop for the whole town, even though he'd started going out to some of the ranches this past year.

Les frowned. Now that he thought about it, he would have expected the woman to have taken her mailbox down by now. Surely she must know how useless it was. And another thing was coming to his mind. The woman hadn't seemed all that familiar with the hardware store the day he'd seen her there, either. Which all added up to only one possibility. "Somebody must be taking the woman's mail to her."

Les looked around. He'd bet it was one of the people sitting right in front of him.

"Well, I don't see what's wrong with that," Elmer finally said defiantly. "I figure it's only neighborly. Besides, it's no trouble to drop their letters in that box. They don't get many of them, anyway. The boy got a letter from Los Angeles, but it wasn't heavy. No two-stamper. And they don't get catalogs to speak of, either. Just the J. C. Penney Christmas catalog."

"The mail is protected by federal law. You shouldn't be touching anyone's mail without their permission." Les wondered if the sheriff's department should put out a book of rules for people. He wondered if anyone in Dry Creek would read it if they did issue one.

Elmer jutted his chin out. "All I'm saying is that there are the two kids, and if we haven't seen them, maybe it's because neither of them needs to go farther than their driveway for the mail. That's all."

"They could even be sick," Linda added softly. "It's flu season. They'd stay inside for sure if they were sick. Maybe they have colds."

"And I can't see sick kids stealing a shepherd," Mrs. Hargrove said. "Especially not in this weather. Their mother probably wouldn't let them go outside if they were sick, and they wouldn't be able to see the Nativity set from the windows in their house, so they wouldn't even know the shepherd was there. They can't steal what they don't even know about, now, can they?"

Les wondered how long the people of Dry Creek would protect a real criminal if one showed up. He hoped he never had to find out. "Forget the shepherd. Nobody said anybody wanted that shepherd. It's the bake set that seems to be the goal. If I remember right, one of those names on the mailbox is Becky. Sounds like a little girl to me. Especially since we know the mother's name is Marla Something-or-the-other."

"It's Marla Gossett. Remember, I told you about her? Said it would be a good idea for you to get acquainted with that new woman," Elmer said as he looked up at Les. "Didn't I say that just the other day?"

Les grunted. "You didn't *say* anything. What you did was break the law by calling in a false fire alarm. That was a crazy stunt. And just to get me over to the hardware store while Mrs. Gossett was there."

"Well, it would have worked if you'd stayed around to talk. She's a nice lady. Charley and I both knew you wouldn't come over if we just said there was an eligible woman we wanted you to meet. When have you ever agreed to do something like that?"

"I have a ranch to run. I can't be running around meeting people all the time."

"Wouldn't hurt you to stop work for a night or two and actually go out on a date," Elmer muttered. "It's not like you're busy with harvest season."

Les had never known the two old men could

be so manipulative. They definitely needed a new checkerboard. And a steak or two to get their blood going.

Les looked directly at Charley and Elmer. "The two of you didn't take that shepherd, did you? Just to give me a reason to talk some more with this Mrs. Gossett?"

The stunned expressions on the faces of the two men were almost comical.

"What would give you that idea?" Elmer demanded.

Les just grunted. He wondered if XIX was part of the telephone number for a dating service.

Charley grinned a little. "Well, this isn't like that. We don't have anything to do with the shepherd being gone."

Les felt a headache coming on. "Maybe it *is* the new people, then. I'll have to go and talk to them."

"Oh, no, you don't. You can't go over there and accuse the Gossetts of taking something," Mrs. Hargrove protested with an indrawn breath. "They're new here. We're supposed to make newcomers feel welcome."

"They're not welcome if they're going to break the law."

"But it's only a plastic shepherd," Linda said

as she looked up from the chair she was sitting in. "You said yourself, it's not like it's a kidnapping."

"It's only a small crime," Charley added with a glance at Mrs. Hargrove. "The women's group didn't even pay real money for it. Just all those soup labels. Hardly counts as a crime, now that I think on it."

That was easily the third time Charley had looked to Mrs. Hargrove for approval in the past ten minutes, and Les knew what that meant. Not only was the sheriff married and off to Maui, but it looked as if Charley was sweet on Mrs. Hargrove. What else would make a man stop speaking his mind until he made sure a particular woman held the same opinion? No, Charley had either turned in his independence or he owed Mrs. Hargrove more money than he could repay.

Les sighed. He didn't know which would be worse. A debt beyond a man's means or one-sided love. Both of them turned a man's spine to mush. It had certainly done that to Charley. One look from Mrs. Hargrove and Charley would probably vote to send that plastic shepherd to the moon on taxpayer money. And Charley was a Republican who didn't believe in spending a dime on anything. Nothing should change a man like that. It just wasn't right. Besides, Mrs. Hargrove looked as if she didn't even know Charley was twisting himself in knots trying to win her approval.

Elmer was the only one who looked as if he was holding on to his common sense.

That was another thing Sheriff Carl Wall had warned Les about. The people of Dry Creek couldn't always be relied upon to see things in an objective manner. For one thing, many of them couldn't bear to see anyone punished. That's why it was so important that the law stood firm. It was for everyone's protection.

"Today it's a plastic shepherd. Tomorrow who knows what it will be," Les said. "We have to stop crime where it starts."

Elmer nodded. "That's right. The law needs to have teeth to it. If the women's group hadn't collected all those soup labels, that Nativity set would have cost five hundred dollars. Who around here has five hundred dollars to throw away?"

There was a moment's silence. Five hundred dollars went a long way in a place like Dry Creek.

"Well, at least take some doughnuts with you if you're going to go over to that house this early in the morning," Linda said as she stepped over to the counter and took the lid off the glass-domed tray that held the doughnuts.

"And be sure and invite the children to Sunday school," Mrs. Hargrove added. She seemed resigned to the fact that someone needed to ask the hard questions. "I've been meaning to go over there with an invitation myself. It just always seems to be snowing every time I think of it, and you know how slippery the streets are when that happens."

"This is a criminal investigation. I'm not going to invite anyone to Sunday school."

Mrs. Hargrove looked at him. "It's the best place for someone to be if they've been stealing. I noticed you weren't in church yourself last Sunday."

"One of my horses threw a shoe and I needed to fix it. You know I'm always there if I can be." Les had come to faith when he was a boy and he lived his commitment. Quietly, of course, but he figured God knew how he felt about public displays of emotion. And even if he didn't dance around and shout hallelujah from the rooftops, he was steady in his faith.

"We miss you in the choir."

"I haven't sung in the choir since I was sixteen."

Mrs. Hargrove nodded. "You still have that voice, though. It's deeper now, but it's just as good. It's a sin to waste a voice like that."

Les had quit the choir when people started to pay too much attention to his singing.

"The Bible doesn't say a man needs to be in the choir." *Or perform in any other public way*, Les added to himself. "It's okay to be a quiet man."

"I know. And you're a good man, Lester Wilkerson. Quiet or not."

He winced. "Make that Les. Lester sounds like my father."

The church had been a home for Les from the day he decided to accept a neighbor's invitation to attend. It was the one place his parents never went, and Les felt he could be himself there.

"I don't know why you never liked the name Lester," Mrs. Hargrove continued. "It's a good old-fashioned name. It's not biblical, of course, but it's been the name of many good men over the years."

"I like Les better. Les Wilkerson."

How did he tell someone like Mrs. Hargrove that he had loved his parents, but he had never respected them? He had never wanted to be his father's son, so he saw no reason to take his first name as well as his last.

Les was a better name for a rancher than Lester, anyway, he thought. He'd changed his name shortly after he'd signed the deed for his place. He had been twenty years old, and that deed had marked his independence from his parents. The name Les helped him begin a new life.

Linda handed him a white bag filled with doughnuts. "I put in some extra jelly ones. Kids always like the jelly ones."

"I wonder if that XIX on the note is the edition number on that bake set," Charley said.

"Maybe it's a clue," Elmer offered. "Is there something that is ten, one and then ten?"

"An *X* sometimes stands for a kiss," Linda said. "You know when people sign their letters XOXO—kisses and hugs."

"I doubt anyone was thinking of kisses." Les figured he didn't have all morning to guess what the numbers meant. Not when he had people to question.

"You might ask the woman to come have dinner with you some night here," Mrs. Hargrove said as Les started to walk to the door. "Just to be sociable. Sort of show her around town."

"Nobody needs a map to get around this town. There's only the one street."

Ever since Charley and Mrs. Hargrove had managed to match up their two children, they had been itching to try their new matchmaking skills on someone else. Well, it wasn't going to be him.

Les would find his own wife when he wanted one and he would do it when no one was watching. He might even have gotten around to asking the new woman out eventually if people had left him alone. She seemed quiet and he liked that. Her brown hair was a very ordinary color. No streaks of auburn. No beauty-parlor waves. It was just always plain and neatly combed when he saw her. She didn't even wear those dangling earrings that always made him feel a woman was prone to changing her opinions from one minute to the next. All in all, he believed, she would be predictable and that was good. Les didn't want an unpredictable wife.

Yes, Marla Gossett might very well have suited him.

Now, of course, he couldn't ask her out. It would be pointless; she'd never accept. Not when he was going to be knocking at her door in a couple of minutes to ask if her daughter was a thief. Only a fool would ask for a date after that, and one thing Les prided himself on was never being a fool.

It was a pity, though. These days Les didn't meet that many quiet women who looked as if they'd make sensible wives. He'd noticed when he saw her in the hardware store that she was a sensible dresser, right down to the shoes she wore. Because of his father, he paid particular attention to a woman's shoes. They told a man a great deal. Still, everything about Mrs. Gossett had seemed practical that day, from her washable cardigan to her well-worn knit pants.

Most men liked a lot of flash in their women. But Les figured the quieter the better. He never really trusted a woman with flash.

Les wondered, just for a moment, if it would be worthwhile to let Mrs. Gossett know he was single, just in case she ever started to wonder about him the way he was wondering about her.

Then he shook his head. He didn't want to chase after an impossible dream. He didn't even know Mrs. Gossett and she didn't know him. What he did know were the reasons he wasn't likely to get to know her. He had to just let the thought go.

Chapter Three

Marla moved the hanging blanket slightly so
she could look out the window of her new living room. The sun would be coming up any
minute, but the small town of Dry Creek was
still dark and quiet. Snow had fallen during
the night and there was just enough light in
the small circle from the one street lamp to
see that there were no fresh tire tracks on the
road going through town.

That didn't mean she could relax and re-
move the blankets, though. Down the street
there was a glow in the window of the café and
she could see several figures through the big
window. People had obviously come into town
from the other direction and any one of them
could decide at any minute to drive down the
road toward her. If they did, they would soon
be able to see inside her front window if she

moved the blanket, and she didn't want anyone to look into her place until she was ready.

The words of her neighbor back in Los Angeles were never far from her mind.

Marla had cleaned her windows with vinegar yesterday and she could still smell the cleaning solution as it mingled with the scent of the mothballs from the blanket. The panes in the windows rattled because the putty was all worn away, but at least they were finally clean.

Today Marla planned to wash the walls. The paint was peeling away and she'd feel better if she knew the walls were brushed down and ready to go when she could afford to buy paint.

In a strange way, she was grateful for the necessity of scrubbing this old house. If it had been less filthy when she arrived here with her children, she might still be brooding over the change she'd made. She'd been nervous the whole trip up here, but now the peeling paint and thick dust called her to action and she had no time to fret.

She had not given any thought to the house until she arrived. If she had not been desperate, she would have turned around and driven away after she first looked inside the door. The house was set back from the street a little and there was a nice white picket fence around it.

That part was how her husband had described the house to her. Marla had been okay with the idea of that white picket fence, but nothing Jorge had said had prepared her for the inside of the house.

Of course, her husband's memories of the house had been from thirty years ago. Jorge wouldn't have recognized the house today, either. Even in their cheap apartment in Los Angeles, the paint had managed to stay on the walls.

Marla didn't want anyone from this small town to look past the fence and into her windows until she was ready. There wasn't much inside her house and, what was there was shabby. On the long drive up, she'd promised herself she would make a proper life for her children in Dry Creek, and she didn't want her relationship with the town to start off with the people here pitying them.

Somewhere around Utah, she'd realized that the ethnic difference was only part of what she needed to worry about. After all, her parents had raised her to be more Anglo than Hispanic, anyway. They'd even given her an Anglo name. She and the children might be able to fit in that way eventually. The fact that they were also poor was another problem. She

knew that from the welfare days of her childhood. A lack of money would be harder to hide
than anything.

Marla planned to get the house in shape before she did more than say a quiet hello to anyone. She didn't want her children to feel shame
for either their heritage or their lack of posses-
sions. First impressions were important.

That's one reason she had hung the plain
khaki-colored blankets over the windows and
left the Mexican striped blankets as coverings
for the sleeping bags.

Maybe if Sammy had had neighbors who
expected good things from him back in Los
Angeles, he wouldn't have been drawn to the
19th Street gang. Of course, the neighbors
were only part of it. She knew she hadn't given
him what he needed, either. She had been so
preoccupied with taking care of Jorge that she
hadn't paid enough attention to Sammy.

It was Sammy who most needed a new start.

Marla took a deep breath of the cool winter air. Despite the fact that the air was tinged
with the scent of vinegar and mothballs, it still
smelled clean and fresh when she compared it
to what she'd breathed down south.

Dry Creek promised a new life for all of
them and Marla intended it to go well. Even

though she'd had car problems on the way up and hadn't had much money left after she'd paid for the repairs, she was determined she and her children were not going to be charity cases. Charity was never free; one always paid the price by enduring the giver's pity. She didn't want that.

She wanted her children to feel proud of who they were.

Besides, they didn't need charity. Any day Marla expected to get a check in the mail refunding the deposit on their apartment. Her rental agreement gave the landlord twenty days to refund the money and he'd probably take all that time. Once she had that check, she would have enough money to buy paint for the walls and a good used sofa. And that was after she put aside enough money to support her family for a few months while she looked for a job. She knew she needed to spend some time with her children before she started a new job, though. Too much had happened too fast in the past year for all of them. They needed time to be together.

At first Marla had worried that she would not have enough money to support her and the children for those few months. It seemed as if the cost of heating the house would take

what little money she had, but then she had discovered that the fireplace in the living room
worked and that there was a seven-foot-high
woodpile half-hidden in the trees behind the
house.

At last, something was going her way.

It looked as if, during the years when the
house had stood empty, the trees had grown
up around the towering stack of log chunks
back there. She hadn't paid any attention to
the stack until the children told her about it
one day and she had gone out to look it over.
The pile had good-sized logs meant for long
winter fires. If need be, on the coldest nights,
she and the children could camp in front of the
fireplace to sleep.

At least heat was one thing that wouldn't re-
quire money for now.

Which was a good thing, because the refund
check was going to total only around a thousand dollars. There wouldn't be much money
left for extras. Christmas this year would be
lean. She'd explained the situation to Sammy
and Becky and they seemed to understand.
Wall paint and a used sofa might not look like
exciting Christmas presents, but it would make
their house more of a home. She was letting
each child pick out the color of the paint for

their bedroom and she was hoping that would be enough of a Christmas present.

Besides, they could make some simple gifts for each other this year. That could be fun for all of them. And she'd make the sweet pork tamales that were the children's favorite. It was her mother's special recipe and that, along with the traditional lighted luminaries, always meant Christmas to Marla.

Marla had brought dozens of corn husks, dried peppers and bags of the cornmeal-like masa with her when she moved to Montana. She remembered the words of the neighbor who had bought her lamp and she didn't want to take any chances. Christmas without tamales was unthinkable, and not just because of the children.

By the time Christmas was here, she hoped to be able to take the blankets off the front windows of her house and welcome any visitors inside. By then, she might even be comfortable offering visitors a tamale and explaining that she and the children had a Hispanic heritage.

Marla saw movement and stopped daydreaming about the future. The door of the café had opened and a man had stepped out. She had recognized the pickup parked next to the café when she first looked out the window, and so she figured the man standing on the café porch was Reserve Deputy Sheriff Les Wilkerson. He was probably getting ready to patrol through Dry Creek and had stopped at the café for coffee. Marla had seen the deputy walk down the street of Dry Creek every morning since she'd moved here and it made her nervous.

She hadn't heard of any criminal activity around, but she kept the children close to the house just in case. She'd called the school when they'd first arrived in Dry Creek and they had agreed, since it had been almost time for the holiday break, that Sammy could start his classes after Christmas. Becky was even more flexible. When she'd first noticed the sheriff patrolling the town, Marla had been glad she'd arranged to have Sammy close by for a few weeks, but maybe if the children were in school she'd at least know more about what was going on.

There must be something happening if a lawman was doing foot patrol. In Los Angeles that happened only in high crime areas. She hadn't heard any gunshots at night, so she doubted robberies were the problem. The deputy must be worried about drugs.

Marla had briefly met the man last Friday

when she was at the hardware store looking for paint, and she had wanted to ask him about any local drug problems. But he had stayed only long enough to scowl at everyone and do something with an ashtray.

The two older men sitting beside the woodstove talked about Les after he left. They made it sound as if he was somebody special. She supposed the older men wanted to reassure her that her children were safe here in Dry Creek with a lawman around, but, truth be told, the reserve deputy didn't make her feel better about the isolation of the small town.

She was used to lawmen, even reserve volunteer lawmen, who had a certain amount of swagger to them. Les didn't strut around at all. He looked strong enough, but he wasn't exactly brawling material. Not only that, he didn't even carry a gun.

She doubted there were any lawmen in Los Angeles who didn't carry a gun. There were certainly none the few times she'd visited her aunts and uncles in Mexico. Marla supposed Les would have to talk a criminal down, but when she'd been introduced to him, he hadn't seemed to be much of a talker. He'd only nodded and mumbled hello to her that day. He was even quieter than she was, and she was perfectly able to carry on a conversation. She'd do fine with talking when she had her house ready for visiting.

Of course, no one else seemed to be worried about Les's lack of conversational skills, and they knew the town and him much better than she did. Maybe he was one of those people who shone in emergency situations, but who didn't appear to be of much use at other times.

Les wasn't even wearing a uniform that day. He'd had cowboy boots on his feet and a plaid flannel shirt on his back. The only thing that had marked him as a reserve deputy sheriff was a vest and, from what the other men said, he didn't even always wear that. Of course, everyone must just know he was the lawman on duty; it was such a small town.

Marla watched Les step off the café porch and start walking down the street. He must be making his usual morning patrol. Fortunately, the sun was starting to lighten up the day, so he might even be able to see while he did it.

Les felt the snow crunch beneath his boots as he moved down the one street in Dry Creek. Usually he thought it was an advantage to have only one street in town. Today, though, he would have liked a million other directions to turn.

He stopped when he got to the church. The Nativity set was still all lit up even though the sun was beginning to rise. The wise men stood to one side with their hands overflowing with gold baubles. The blond angel was hanging from a wire attached to the rain gutters of the church. Les took a minute to look closely at the rain gutters and note that whoever had written the note was right. Someone did need to add another wire or the angel would eventually fall.

Les looked back at the wise men and wondered why one of them hadn't been taken instead of the lone shepherd. They certainly looked more exciting than the missing figure. Everyone he knew, except himself, would pick flash over something drab any day. Strangely, it didn't make him feel any easier in his mind about the theft.

When he could delay no longer, Les walked farther down the street and then started up the path to the Gossett house. Until Marla and her children moved to town, the house had been closed up. Old man Gossett had spent some time in prison before he died and no one had taken care of the house. Someone had enough civic pride to paint part of the picket fence that faced the street so the property looked somewhat cared for if an outsider happened to look at it on a casual drive through town. None of the people in Dry Creek liked to see the town buildings look neglected and Les couldn't blame them.

As he walked up the path, Les saw how the weather had started to flake the white paint off the house until there were large sections of exposed gray boards. Even the snowdrifts couldn't disguise the fact that the yard had gone to seed. Only the pine trees in the back of the house had flourished, growing together in thick clumps of muted green.

Les was halfway up the walk when someone turned off the light inside the house. For the first time, Les thought maybe the little girl really had stolen the shepherd. What else but guilt would make someone turn off the lights when a visitor was coming to the door? Usually people turned a light on when someone was walking toward their house.

When Les stepped on the porch, the door opened a crack. It was just enough for Les to see a small portion of a woman's face. There was one brown eye and a hand holding the side of the door. The hand covered up most of what face would have shown in the crack. The room behind the face was in darkness. Les wouldn't have recognized the woman even though he had met her that day in the hardware store.

"Mrs. Gossett?"

The woman nodded.

Les wished she would open the door wider. Regardless of what he'd told himself, he was looking forward to seeing more of the woman's face. He hadn't taken a very good look at her the other day in the hardware store and he'd like to see her better. There was no particular reason to ask her to open the door wider, though. Especially because it was cold out and she was probably just keeping her heat inside like any wise Montana housewife would do.

"I brought something to eat," Les said as he held up the white bag. "For the kids. And you, of course."

He had a feeling he could express himself a lot better if the woman didn't keep eyeing him as if she was going to slam the door in his face any minute now.

At his words, her face stiffened even more. "We have enough to eat. You don't need to worry about us."

Les had coaxed frightened kittens out of their hiding places many times and he reminded himself that patience usually won out over fear.

"It's only a few doughnuts," Les forced his voice to be softer. "Linda, at the café, thought the kids might like them."

The woman's face relaxed some. "Well, I guess doughnuts are different."

The woman opened the door and Les gave her the bag. He waited a minute in hopes she was going to ask him inside. It would be easier to talk to her if she was relaxed and not looking at him through the crack in the door. But once she took the bag, she closed the door so it was back in its original position.

"Please tell the woman—Linda—thank you for us. We haven't had a chance to get over to the café yet, but it's a very nice gesture."

Les was afraid the woman was going to think he had just come by to bring her the doughnuts, so he said his piece. "I'm doing a search of houses. We've had some property stolen from the church."

The woman frowned. "We don't go to church."

The woman turned a little as if she heard something inside the house.

"You don't need to go to church to take something."

The woman snapped back to look at him. "Are you accusing me of stealing? From a church?"

"No, ma'am." Les ran his finger around his shirt collar. "It's just that I did think that maybe your daughter—well, do you know where your daughter was last night?"

The woman turned again to look inside the house.

Les figured it was one of the children who had been distracting the woman, so he wasn't surprised when he heard her whisper to someone. "Just be patient. Mommy will be right there."

The woman turned back to look at Les. In all of the turning, the door had opened a little farther. "Becky was here with me last night."

The woman was wearing an old beige robe that was zipped up to her neck and she didn't have any makeup on her face. She had strong bones, Les noticed. And a weariness to her that made him think she'd come through a long patch of hard times. He couldn't let his sudden sympathy for her change what he needed to do, though.

"Was your daughter with you for the entire night?" Les could see into the rest of the large room behind the woman. The windows were all covered so the room was in shadows, but he could make out most of it. Not that there was much to see. Except for a wooden sitting chair, there was nothing there. Maybe the family's furniture was still coming on a moving truck.

"Of course, all night. Where else would she be?" The woman was looking straight at him now. "I don't even know why you're asking me these questions. You came straight to my door. I saw you. You're not asking everybody. Just because we don't have blond hair and blue eyes like everyone else around here, it doesn't mean we stole something."

"No, of course not." Les was bewildered. Did everyone around here have blond hair? He hadn't noticed. Still, he'd come to do a job and he might as well get it done. "I'm talking to people because someone stole one of the Nativity figures from the set in front of the church."

"That has nothing to do with us."

Les nodded. "I just wondered, because whoever took the figure wanted to trade it back to the church for a Suzy bake set."

A little girl's squeal came from behind the door. Les couldn't see the girl, but he could hear her as she said, "A Suzy bake set! The one with the cupcakes?"

"No, dear, I don't think so," the woman said with her face turned to the inside of the room.

Why was it that the line of a woman's neck, when she turned to look over her shoulder, always reminded him of a ballet dancer? Les asked himself. Marla—well, Mrs. Gossett—had a beautiful neck.

The woman turned back to look at Les. She even gave him a small smile, which made the knot in his stomach relax. No one who was guilty would smile. But then, maybe the mother didn't know what the daughter had done.

The woman continued, "I'm sorry. I think every little girl everywhere wants that Suzy bake set in the cupcake edition. It's quite the thing. I don't know if you can even find it in the stores anymore."

Les nodded. Maybe that's why someone had written the demand note. Maybe they thought the church would have extra pull with a store. "Whoever took the shepherd left a note." He held the paper out to her. "I think a girl might have written it."

The woman didn't even look up to read the note. She just shook her head. "If that's where you're headed, you should know my daughter is only four. She can't even write her name."

"Oh." Les had not known the girl was so young. He didn't think a girl that age could even lift the shepherd figure. The thing was plastic, but it was heavy enough. And it was bulky.

"She's going to learn to write her name," the woman continued, as if she was making a point. "We believe in schooling. She'll go to preschool a couple of days a week in Miles City after the holidays. Most kids here probably already know how to write their names, but Becky didn't get a chance to go to preschool in Los Angeles. If she's behind, she'll catch up."

"I'm sure she'll learn to write in no time," Les said just to put the woman at ease, since her daughter's schooling seemed important to her. "Kids learn fast."

Les hoped he was speaking the truth. What did he know about kids? He knew he should forget about the kids and say goodbye, but he found he didn't want to rush off. Not now that, with the sun fully up and spreading its sunshine all over, Les noticed that some of the shadows were gone from the woman's face.

He wondered if she would go out to dinner with him after all. Now that they were talking about education instead of crime, she seemed a little friendlier.

"I—ah—" Les swallowed. "We have a good school in Miles City. You don't need to worry about that."

The woman smiled. "I'm glad to know that."

Les wasn't prepared for the woman's full smile.

He swallowed again. "Thanks for talking to me. Let me know if you see anything suspicious. It's probably just some kids playing a prank. Wanting to see if I can figure out that XIX clue they left. I wonder if it's part of a math equation."

Les had been ready to turn and walk away when the smile fell from Mrs. Gossett's face and something in her eyes shifted. She'd suddenly gone tense.

"Is there something you want to tell me?" he asked.

She shook her head. The weariness was back on her face. "The XIX. Where was that?"

"At the end of the note."

The woman bit her lip nervously. "Are you going to be in town for a little while?"

Les didn't flatter himself that she wanted to see him again, but he nodded. "I'll be at the café for another half hour or so. If you think of something that might help, let me know."

She nodded.

There wasn't anything more to say, so Les gave her a goodbye nod. "It was a pleasure to talk with you, ma'am. And welcome to Dry Creek."

Les turned and left. He hoped Mrs. Hargrove would be happy with his little welcome speech at the end. He'd even meant it.

Marla barely waited for the man to step off her porch before she closed the door and locked it. Of course, turning the lock was just habit. She had nothing to fear from the reserve deputy sheriff. Although, if her suspicions were right, she might not want to hear what he had to say to her and her children if she had to take her son over to the café in a few minutes.

"Sammy," she called.

Becky was happily walking around with her bunny slippers and frog pajamas on. But it was almost seven o'clock and Marla hadn't heard from her son yet this morning. Usually he was up by now even though it wasn't a school day. She'd thought earlier that he was sleeping in. Now she knew he was just hiding out.

"Sammy, come out here."

Marla leaned back against the locked door and looked around. For the first time she wondered how she could have fooled herself so completely. She could paint the rooms in her house with gold leaf and the people here wouldn't respect them. Not if Sammy had stolen the Nativity shepherd from the church and tagged that note with the 19th Street gang symbol. Her family would be marked as troublemakers regardless of how their house looked or what their ethnic background was. People were scared of gangs, and rightfully so. If they figured out Sammy had wanted to be in a gang, there would be no new start for them. The whole move up here would have been pointless.

"Sammy!"

Her son stepped into the living room. He was wearing a long white T-shirt and baggy pants. It was typical gang clothes for south central L.A.

"I thought you were going to throw those clothes away," Marla said. They didn't have many clothes, but Sammy did have some jeans that fit better. And why did he need to spike his hair?

"I've got to wear something." Sammy glared at her. "I can't go around naked."

Marla felt that sometimes she didn't recognize her son. "You have those jeans I got for you to wear when you start school here—"

"They don't fit." Sammy shrugged. "I'm saving them for when we paint the house."

Marla forced herself to relax. She supposed that clothes were the least of her worries, although people did form opinions about young people because of the way they were dressed. "I just want to be proud of you."

Sammy grunted. "What's in the bag?"

Marla looked down. Becky was sitting on the floor and had already opened the white bag Les had left with them. She hadn't taken anything out, although she had a grin on her face.

There were so few smiling moments for Becky these days that Marla didn't want to spoil this one by questioning Sammy right now. The sheriff would be in town for another half hour. They had time to eat a bite.

"The woman at the café sent us over doughnuts for breakfast." Marla said. "Wasn't that nice of her?"

Becky nodded and beamed up at her. "Yes, Mommy."

Sammy grunted.

Marla didn't react to Sammy. Gratitude wasn't the big problem of the day, either. "Let's go sit at the table when we eat them. We don't want to get everything sticky."

Sammy had already walked over and looked

in the sack Becky held. For the first time this morning he reminded Marla of the little boy he had been. "Hey, there's jelly doughnuts. Cool. I can see the raspberry filling coming out of one of them."

"Let's take them to the table," Marla repeated for Becky's ears.

"I am, Mommy," Becky said as she stood up and then reached down and grabbed the bag.

Marla watched her children walk into the kitchen together. Becky was holding the bag of doughnuts, but Marla could see that Sammy was guarding them as he walked with his sister. What was she to do? Marla asked herself as she leaned back against the door. Sammy's heart was good. Look how careful he was to help Becky without taking the sack from her. An aggressive child would just grab the bag. But not Sammy. He had always had a warm place in his heart for his little sister.

She was surprised it hadn't all clicked together for her earlier when she was standing there talking to the deputy sheriff. Becky might not have written that note asking for a Suzy bake set, but Sammy had. He knew what Becky wanted for Christmas. Becky had been talking about that bake set for weeks. Marla had even wondered if she might be able to

squeeze the money out of her budget for one.
She hadn't been sure if she could do it, so she
hadn't said anything to either of the children.
She'd just let her suggestion of handmade gifts
stand.

Maybe that had been a mistake. Marla realized that if she had told Sammy she was buying a few presents after all, maybe he wouldn't
have taken that shepherd. Somewhere in all of
this, she was partially at fault.

She couldn't help but think that Jorge would
have known what to do for Sammy. Maybe
Sammy felt free to misbehave because he
knew she wasn't as sure of herself as Jorge
had been in disciplining him. She wasn't used
to flying solo as a parent and she wasn't sure
she could do a good job of it. Sometimes a
growing boy needed a father.

Marla listened to the voices of her children
in the dining room for a minute, then started
forward to join them. She was going to have
to do her best to give Sammy what a father
would.

Marla was glad the card table and folding
chairs had fit in the luggage carrier on top of
the car when she moved up here. Her children
were sitting at the table now. It might not be as
sturdy as the table she would eventually buy

for them, but it was important for them to have a place to sit down and eat together. For all of Sammy's sullen ways, he'd never protested eating dinner with the family.

Sammy had put white paper plates and plastic cups on the table. He'd even brought out the gallon of milk. Marla was pleased that they had waited for her.

Marla let everyone finish their doughnuts before she cleared her throat.

"Becky, will you go to your room and get dressed, please?"

Becky didn't always end up with a matching outfit, but she liked to dress herself and Marla encouraged her to be independent.

After Becky left, Marla turned to Sammy. "Is there something you need to tell me?"

"Nah," Sammy muttered, his face flushing.

Marla counted to three. "Did you take a shepherd from the church's Nativity scene?"

Sammy's face got redder. "It's just a stupid shepherd. They don't even exist anymore. At least, not anywhere except in Mexico. I mean, who needs them? We're through with that life. We're turning white."

Marla kept her voice even. "Just because we moved up here, it doesn't mean that we're not still part Hispanic."

Sammy grunted. "I haven't seen any *amigos* around."

No one would know Sammy was Hispanic by looking at him. She knew he identified himself with his old *amigos*, but maybe it was time for them all to step away from their background a little bit.

"You'll meet some new friends when you go to school."

"Yeah, right."

"We're not ashamed of being Hispanic." Marla tried again. "We're just getting to know people slow and easy. We don't need to be any particular ethnic group for a while."

Sammy grunted.

Marla decided she couldn't talk about their heritage all morning.

"You know it's wrong to take things that don't belong to you. We'll go over to the café and talk to the deputy who was here asking about the shepherd. Then you'll give the shepherd back and we'll talk about what your punishment will be."

Marla was hoping that if Sammy confessed to what he had done and returned the shepherd, no charges would be filed. She didn't know how much the Nativity figure was worth, but she doubted it had a high enough value to make this anything but a misdemeanor. Once they figured that out, she'd talk more with Sammy about his other feelings.

"I could give up Christmas," Sammy offered. "Not that it's going to be anything, anyway."

"I'm hoping to make sweet pork tamales," Marla said.

Sammy looked up. "With the green chilies?"

Marla nodded. "If I can find a nice pork roast to use in the filling."

"Well, maybe I could give up Christmas after the tamales are all gone."

Marla smiled. "We'll talk."

Marla wondered how she could make Sammy feel more at home in Dry Creek. She knew he missed his friends. Even though those friends were not good for him, he was still entitled to miss them. A few days ago he'd gotten a letter from a boy back in Los Angeles. Sammy had protested, but eventually he'd agreed to let her read the note about some baseball, his lucky baseball, that he'd left behind and how the boy was going to get it to him soon.

At least Sammy had one friend there who didn't sound like a gang member. She hoped baseball wasn't gang code for something else.

She couldn't forbid Sammy to have contact with everybody, though. A boy needed some friends, and the note sounded fine. Maybe she had been wrong to postpone school for him by the few weeks that she had. Of course, it was too late to change that now. The classes would be on Christmas break next week, anyway.

"Let's see if Becky is ready," Marla said. "We want to go over while the sheriff is at the café."

"He's not a regular lawman, is he?" Sammy asked with a frown. "He doesn't look like the police or anything."

"I suspect he's close enough to the real thing."

"I'm not afraid of him," Sammy announced.

Marla figured her son was lying about not being afraid when he took Becky's hand to hold while they walked down the street to the café. He shrugged off the hand Marla tried to rest on his shoulder, but she was glad he had Becky's hand at least.

They had to pass the church to reach the café and Marla looked over at the Nativity set. Since the church was on the same side of the road as her house, she couldn't see the lighted figures from her windows. It was nice just knowing they were there, though. She'd heard someone say that the whole town of Dry Creek planned to sing carols around the Nativity set on Christmas Eve.

Marla hadn't taken her children to church here yet, and once everyone knew what Sammy had done they might not be welcome, anyway, especially not if they made the gang connection. But she hoped they would at least be able to hear the carols being sung. Listening to Christmas carols took Marla back to her childhood.

During some of their poorest years as a family, the best part of Christmas for her had been sneaking into the back of a church and listening to the singing. Her life seemed brandnew every Christmas when she heard those songs. After a few carols, she didn't care that her only gift was whatever came in the charity basket from whatever group had been assigned her family. She'd never joined a church or anything, but she somehow knew that the world had been changed forever on that first Christmas night.

She had put that wooden cross up in her bedroom at the new house and, if she wasn't sleeping by the fireplace that night, she would study it before she turned off her light. Her husband had found some peace by looking at the cross, but so far that peace continued to elude her. The only thing she felt when she looked at it was longing. Longing for security. Longing for a better life for her children. Longing for things she could not even name.

Marla could see the sheriff through the café window. He was sitting at a table waiting. She didn't know whether to be relieved or disappointed that he was still there. She knew Sammy needed to acknowledge what he had done, but she hoped the sheriff wouldn't make the connection to the 19th Street gang. Somehow the sheriff had seemed more intimidating to her this morning than he had when she'd first met him in the hardware store.

She wondered if she should tell him about Sammy's feelings for his old friends. Maybe the man had once been the odd one out like Sammy was these days. He was a strange one, that man. He looked so quiet, but something in his eyes said he saw everything. She hadn't noticed it until this morning. Would he see what was behind a boy's vandalism? She could only hope for mercy if he did.

Chapter Four

Les was on his second cup of coffee. He was sitting in the café hoping Mrs. Gossett would come by and tell him what she suspected about the missing shepherd. He'd already answered the questions of everyone waiting for him back in the café and he was getting tired of lingering when he had work to do.

"So she didn't say *anything* about the shepherd?" Charley asked him again.

Charley, Mrs. Hargrove and Elmer were sitting at the table next to him, watching him drink coffee. Les would feel more comfortable if they'd take their focus off him, but he couldn't tell people where to look. He supposed it all went with the job, anyway. They were curious, and he didn't have the gift of chatter. But maybe he should try.

Les shook his head and cleared his throat.

"I don't think she knew anything about it before I told her. At least, that's how she acted."

He felt comfortable saying that much. He wouldn't mention the expression that had come over the woman's face when she had time to think about the Suzy bake set for a moment or two. When she thought about it, she had suspected something. He could see it in her eyes; they had turned from annoyed to scared in a heartbeat. He wasn't going to make his suspicions public, however. He knew how fast gossip could spread and he didn't want the family tried and convicted before they even had a chance to talk to anyone about the whole situation. Besides, he could be wrong.

"Another refill?" Linda asked as she walked by his table.

"I better not." Les looked at his watch. He'd been sitting here for almost thirty minutes. He'd give it another five. He still had those cows to feed. Besides, he was beginning to feel foolish waiting for someone who wasn't showing up.

"Here they come," Elmer announced. He'd positioned himself so he could look out the café window and see the road to the left. "A boy, a little girl and the mother. They look serious, too."

Les felt his neck knot up. "Maybe we shouldn't all be sitting here waiting for them."

"Oh." Elmer shuffled his chair around so it wasn't facing the window.

"Let me get my knitting out," Mrs. Hargrove said as she lifted her bag up to the table and started to rummage around in it.

"I could go over to the counter and get me a doughnut," Charley announced as he stood up.

"Get me one, too?" Elmer asked.

Les wasn't sure what was worse—the sudden staged activity or the stares that would have faced the family otherwise.

"I need to get a fresh pot of coffee," Linda said as she started walking back to the kitchen.

Les deliberately did not turn around in his chair, so that he continued facing away from the door. He didn't even turn when he heard the click of the door opening and felt the rush of cold air on his neck. He believed in giving people some room to move. And he could not be sure that Marla Gossett was here to talk to him. Maybe she had walked over here with her children so they could thank Linda for the doughnuts.

Les could almost feel someone looking at him. He wished now that he'd turned around before the family entered the café.

"Sheriff Wilkerson," the woman finally said.

He turned in his chair, trying, and probably failing, to look natural.

He hadn't expected them to be huddled together. The woman looked frightened.

"You can call me Les."

"Could we talk to you outside?" The woman stood beside the boy.

This was the first time Les had gotten a chance to look at the boy. If he'd seen him before, he would have made the connection earlier that he was the one who had taken the shepherd. The boy had a sullen look on his face that reminded Les of himself at that age. He had on a wrinkled white T-shirt that was too big for him and his hair looked as if it had tried to face down a tornado and failed.

The boy hadn't been out of bed for long and Les wondered if he just hadn't had time to do things like comb his hair. Most likely it wasn't a matter of the time of day. The boy would probably still look that way at noon. Les guessed life was not going the way the boy wanted it to and likely it hadn't been for some time now. He wouldn't be the first kid in that situation to steal something. Les might have turned to petty crime himself if he hadn't found a church at that age instead. A boy needed to belong to something that challenged him, whether it was a sports team or a youth group.

Les stood up. "I'm just on my way out, anyway."

"You and the kids come back in and have breakfast when you've finished with Les here," Mrs. Hargrove offered with a smile for Marla. "My treat."

Mrs. Hargrove had her knitting in her lap and her needles in her hand.

"I'm sorry, but we can't," Marla said. She didn't want to discourage the woman's friendliness. "Maybe some other morning. We have a lot of things to do today."

"At least stop for coffee and orange juice," Linda added with another smile. She was holding a pot of coffee. "I just made some fresh coffee. That doesn't take much time and it's on the house."

"You've already given us the doughnuts." Marla put a hand on each child's shoulder even though Sammy scowled up at her. "I hope you'll let me pay for them."

"Absolutely not."

Marla nodded. "Well, then, we appreciate them. Don't we, children?"

Marla squeezed each child's shoulder and they each murmured something.

In that instant, Marla had a flashback to the times when her mother had done the same awkward thing to her and she'd had to mumble her gratitude to the latest person who had taken pity on their family. It was still hard for her to say thank-you when someone did something nice for her. It was always worse when she had to say thank-you to a charity person.

Marla wondered if her mother had felt as overwhelmed being a single parent after her father died as she did. Still, next time she'd refuse the doughnuts. The price of charity was too high. Not that there was likely to be a repeat of the gesture, not when people found out that Sammy had taken the church's shepherd.

"Well, thank you again," Marla said as she turned. She was only now getting used to the heat in the café. It was cold outside, but she had no desire to have the conversation with the sheriff where it would be overheard by others. She didn't think there was much chance that the news of Sammy's theft would stay a secret in this small town, but she had to try. She didn't want to see the way people would look at her and the children after they knew what Sammy had done. Still, those looks would be

better than what they'd receive if people put
the clues together and figured out that Sammy
gave his allegiance to a Hispanic street gang.

The deputy sheriff was already standing
over by the door.

"Thanks," Marla said as the deputy sheriff
opened the door for her and the children.

The winter air was cold, but Marla waited
for the man to close the door and turn to face
her and the children before she began. "Sammy
has something to say to you."

The deputy sheriff squatted down a little so
that he was at Sammy's height. "I'm listening."

Marla still had her hand on Sammy's
shoulder and she could feel her son tense up.
Whether it was because she had her hand on
his shoulder or the deputy sheriff made him
nervous she didn't know.

"That whole Nativity thing is stupid. Shepherds don't even exist anymore."

"Sammy," Marla said softly. "We don't say
things are stupid. Besides, that's not what we
came here to say."

The boy's chin jutted out and he was silent.

Marla wondered if she was going to have to
confess on her son's behalf.

Instead, the deputy sheriff started to talk.
"Well, I know one real shepherd who would

disagree with you. I'll introduce you some time. I have some sheep myself. Even a few little lambs."

Sammy looked up at that, but didn't say anything.

The sheriff continued, "I wanted to thank you for calling our attention to that wire. If we hadn't seen it, the angel would have fallen. We'll have someone take care of it."

Sammy glared at the deputy sheriff. "It doesn't matter if an angel falls. It's supposed to be able to fly, anyway, isn't it?"

The man chuckled. "I'm afraid our angel isn't quite up to that yet."

Marla had forgotten that Becky was listening until her daughter spoke. "Maybe that's what the shepherd did. Maybe he flew away."

Marla decided she needed to do something before Les Wilkerson thought they were all crazy. "Sammy."

Sammy looked up at her rebelliously for a moment and then lowered his gaze. "Nothing flew away. I took it."

Everyone was quiet.

"Was there any particular reason?" the deputy sheriff finally asked thoughtfully. "I know the church will work with you if—"

"I just took it, okay?"

The deputy sheriff nodded. "You know it's considered stealing?"

"So arrest me already." Sammy still looked defiant.

"Oh, surely, you won't arrest him?" Marla spoke in a rush. "He's only eleven. I know it's wrong, but—"

The deputy sheriff held up his hand. "Nobody's talking about arresting him."

"He'll bring it back." Marla turned to her son. "Won't you, Sammy?"

Sammy stared straight ahead for a minute before he nodded.

"Well, we appreciate that," the deputy sheriff said. "People have been looking forward to having that Nativity scene outside the church when they sing carols on Christmas Eve. It just wouldn't be the same without the shepherd."

"I said I'd bring it back," Sammy said.

The man nodded. "Then we can talk about what kind of consequences there should be for what you did."

"He'll be punished," Marla said in a rush. Maybe the deputy sheriff wasn't going to tell everyone about the theft. Maybe they had a chance at a new life in this town after all. "You don't need to worry about that. I'm taking away his television privileges. And he'll have extra chores to do."

They didn't have much of a television, but Sammy did like watching sports on it.

"Maybe he should do some chores for the church, too," the man said.

"Of course," Marla agreed. "He could sweep the floors or maybe clean some windows."

She didn't know what she would tell people about why Sammy was doing any of those things, but she would think of something without making it sound as if he was doing any good deeds.

"He could always help Mrs. Hargrove with her Sunday-school class," the deputy sheriff added thoughtfully. "She has a lot of first graders and she's always looking for extra help when they practice for the Christmas program."

Marla saw all the color drain out of Sammy's face. Well, the lawman had finally gotten her son's attention.

"Is that like *babysitting*?" Sammy asked, his horror evident. "Would people see me?"

"Well, people would need to see you," the deputy sheriff said calmly. "You might even need to stand up and sing with the kids when they do their piece in the program. They're the angel choir."

"But I'm too tall," Sammy said quickly. "They'd all be baby angels. And I don't have blond hair."

"I think you'll do all right," the man said. "I'm sure Mrs. Hargrove has a pair of wings that are large enough for you. And there will be all different colors of hair in the angel choir."

"I'd have to wear wings? In front of people?"

The lawman nodded seriously. "With gold glitter on them. The kids make the wings in class, so you'll be able to make yours really sparkle. You probably remember how to cut with those little scissors."

Sammy was starting to turn a little green.

"And a halo," the deputy sheriff continued with a straight face. "I don't know if you'll wear sheets or bathrobes yet, but Mrs. Hargrove will figure that out. You'll need to be in something white."

"I want a halo," Becky said happily as she hung on to Marla's coat.

Marla patted Becky's head without answering.

Her son looked shell-shocked.

"But the first order of business is to bring

the shepherd back where he belongs," the man said. "Do you need help in getting him back?"

Sammy shook his head.

"He'll bring the shepherd back right away," Marla said. "And if there's any damage, we'll fix it."

The shepherd was plastic and Marla realized Sammy might have scratched some of its paint off here or there. If he had, they'd paint over the scratches until the shepherd was as good as new.

"Oh, I'm sure the thing's in fine shape," the deputy sheriff said. "Sammy here knows he'll have even more chores to do if something happens to it."

The boy swallowed and then nodded.

"You're sure you don't need any help bringing it back?" the deputy sheriff asked again. "It's kind of big."

Sammy shook his head. "I'm big, too."

Marla waited for her son to walk off the porch and head back to their house. She wanted to talk to the deputy sheriff for a minute, anyway, without Sammy overhearing her.

"Thank you," Marla said when Sammy was halfway to their house. She looked up at the man. She didn't know why she'd ever thought he wasn't confident enough to be a lawman.

He looked completely in control. "I appreciate you talking to my son."

The man nodded. "It's my job."

For the first time, Marla noticed that the man had a tan line on his forehead. The cold air gave the bottom part of his face a red tinge, but his forehead, which had no tan, was even whiter than it had been inside the café. She wondered if it was really his job to have conversations outside in below-freezing temperatures just to save a young boy's pride.

"And I promise I'll talk to Sammy again myself," Marla continued. She looked the man in the eye so he would know she was serious. "He's not a bad kid. He's just trying to get adjusted to a new place. And he misses his old friends."

"I can understand that. It's hard when a kid moves around."

Marla took a deep breath. "This is a final move for us. We want to make this our home."

"I'm glad."

Marla watched the man's face to see if he was being sarcastic. After what he had just found out about Sammy, she would be surprised if any lawman would welcome them into their community. But there was nothing but friendliness in the man's eyes. Of course, he didn't know Sammy's biggest goal was to be in a street gang.

"Thank you," Marla said. She let a few moments pass. "I, ah, I was wondering if you were going to tell anyone about Sammy taking the shepherd?"

"Well, there's no official record of it, if that's what you mean. He won't have a police record or anything."

"Oh." Marla hadn't even thought about that. She'd just been worried about the community gossip. "That's good."

"No one here knows that it was Sammy," the man continued. "I'm hoping we can wrap it up before any more people even know that the shepherd is missing."

Marla nodded. "Thank you. It's just that, with the kids—"

The man held up his hand. "I know how sensitive boys that age can be about everyone talking about them."

Marla stood on the porch and thought how nice it was that the deputy sheriff genuinely did seem to understand. Maybe Sammy would benefit from talking to a man like this one. The only advice anyone had given to her on how to be a solo parent was to suggest she find a man who would relate to her son. They meant someone like an uncle or a grandfather, and she had dismissed the idea because the only relatives she had left were in Mexico and she didn't want to send Sammy down to them. But seeing this man today made her wonder. Maybe someone besides a relative would be willing to help Sammy.

She gave up the thought as soon as it passed through her mind. She could not ask the man standing in front of her to take on Sammy's problems. He was having this conversation with her only because it was his job, anyway. She should just say thank-you and let the man get back to work.

She didn't have a chance to say anything, though, because she heard a rumble start. At first she thought it sounded like some kind of distant thunder. Then there was a loud crack. But that didn't make any sense. There were no clouds in the sky and it was snow weather, not rain weather.

The deputy sheriff didn't wait to figure out what the sound was. He started running toward it.

Marla heard the café door open behind her, but she didn't turn to see who had come out. Instead, she grabbed Becky's hand and followed the deputy sheriff as fast as she could with her daughter beside her. When he turned into her driveway, she knew for certain that the sound was from her house. Or, at least, from near her house.

But what would make a noise like that? She hadn't hooked up the gas furnace yet, so she knew it wasn't a gas explosion. The roof didn't look as if it had caved in and no windows appeared to be broken. In fact, it had sounded like something falling instead of exploding.

Becky couldn't keep up, so Marla let go of her daughter's hand when she was inside their front fenced yard. She was safe here.

"Follow Mommy," Marla whispered as she started running faster.

She still heard footsteps and, hopefully, one of the people following her would see to Becky. Marla was scared. Whatever had fallen could have hurt Sammy. She should have asked him where he had hid the shepherd instead of just asking him to bring it back. A father would have known to ask that of a young boy.

Marla had just assumed her son had hidden the shepherd in some nice safe place. A father would have suspected otherwise. Maybe some women could be good fathers to their sons, but she was not one of them. She was a failure as a single parent, and Sammy was paying the price.

Chapter Five

Les saw the woodpile as soon as he rounded the corner of the house. Of course, his eyes didn't go to the woodpile as much as they went to the boy standing precariously on the half of the stack that had not tumbled to the ground ten seconds ago.

The cut logs that hadn't fallen were likely to go at any minute. And if they did, Sammy would fall with them.

"Don't move," Les said softly as he forced himself to stop and take a deep breath. Les didn't want to panic the boy any more than he already was. "We'll get you down—just hold yourself steady."

Les heard the sound of footsteps behind him and he held up a hand without turning around. He didn't know what noise would do to the balance of those old cut logs, but the fewer people walking close to the wood the better it would be.

Les took a step toward Sammy. "Do you ever play football?"

"Yeah, sometimes."

Les took a few more steps until he was close enough so that Sammy could see his eyes. "Good. That's good."

Les steadied himself, all the while locking into Sammy's gaze. They would need coordination to make his plan work. And trust. Sammy needed to trust him. "Have you ever tried a flying tackle on someone?"

"Of course," Sammy said. "I'm not a baby."

"No, no, you're not, son," Les said as he took a step closer yet.

"I'm not your son," Sammy said.

Les held out his arms. "I want you to pretend you're taking a flying tackle and aim yourself right at my chest."

If the boy tried to jump straight down, Les was afraid the pressure on the logs would cause another slide, toppling both of them. They might not die, but they'd have some broken bones.

"Now?"

Les kept his eyes on Sammy's. He could see the fear in the boy, but he could see some bravery, as well. It was too bad the boy had lost his father. Even now he could tell how sensitive the boy was to that fact. Most boys would have let the son remark slide. For all the embarrassment his parents had caused him, Les was still glad neither of them had died young, as Sammy's dad had done.

Les nodded. "Now."

Marla bit her lip as she listened to the deputy sheriff and her son. She didn't want to call out and make Sammy fall, but she could barely stand to keep silent. She stood at the corner of the house, careful not to go any closer. She didn't want Sammy to look at her instead of the man. The air was cold on her face. She knew because she'd blinked away a tear and it felt warm sliding down her cheek. She wasn't close enough to see if there were any tears on Sammy's face.

She wished she'd spent more time in this overgrown area behind the house instead of worrying about what people saw in the front of the house. Maybe if she had, she'd have wondered about what would happen if moisture got inside that tall stack of firewood and then someone stood, or even jumped, on top of it. The early snow here had been heavy enough with moisture to make all of those logs slick.

She knew that from the log pieces they had brought inside the house to use in the fireplace.

If she'd been paying more attention, maybe she would have either braced the wood up or pulled it down to size. If her husband were still alive, he would have noticed and done something about it.

Her son looked so small. He had his legs braced on top of the woodpile, and Marla could almost see him draw in his breath. She hoped the deputy sheriff knew what he was doing.

Suddenly she noticed those baggy pants Sammy was wearing and wished she had insisted he change into the ones that fit better. All of that loose denim could catch on a log and make him trip instead of jump. That would be disastrous.

Marla felt someone put a hand on her arm and she looked over to see Mrs. Hargrove at her side. The older woman had Becky with her and several others behind her.

"I've been praying," Mrs. Hargrove whispered to Marla as she squeezed her arm. "Your son's in God's hands."

Marla nodded. She wasn't one to deny other people their faith. She had her wooden cross, but she'd never actually prayed to God. She didn't even know much about people who claimed to talk to God.

Of course, there were a lot of things she didn't know much about. Science. Art history. Latin. She always figured she could learn what she needed to know about any of those things when the time came. She should have started learning about prayer after Jorge died, however. She believed Jorge had come to some faith in the end. She should have explored that.

Now she wished she'd gone to a church and tried to at least learn a thing or two about prayer. Fortunately, Mrs. Hargrove seemed to know what she was doing. At least, the older woman seemed confident.

"Thank you," Marla whispered.

Sammy bent his knees slightly and arched himself into space. Just like that.

Marla's heart stopped beating as she saw her son's body sail. *Please, God*, she breathed. Then she saw him hit the deputy sheriff in the chest. The deputy let Sammy knock him to the ground, but as he fell the man folded Sammy into him and rolled them both away from the woodpile.

"Thank you," Marla whispered again as another tear slid down her cheek. She didn't know if she was thanking God or Mrs. Hargrove or the deputy sheriff or all three of them.

The woodpile shook slightly, then the logs that were still in place began to crash down. Marla noticed the deputy sheriff had moved Sammy and himself even farther away from the falling pieces of wood. They were safe.

Mrs. Hargrove let go of Marla's arm. "My word! That was something."

Marla wiped away another tear. "I'm going to give Sammy a talking-to he won't forget."

"I bet it feels like he's taken ten years off your life. Thank God Lester was here to help. That man has a sense of balance like something you've never seen. Used to be quite the football player around here—until he quit playing, that is."

Marla nodded. She appreciated the sound of Mrs. Hargrove's voice. It made everything slow down a little. She'd have to remember to thank the deputy sheriff. She was glad she'd never voiced any of her reservations about his abilities to keep Dry Creek safe. She looked over at where the man stood with Sammy now and wondered what she had been worried about earlier. She was sure the deputy sheriff could protect Dry Creek from anything.

Becky walked around Mrs. Hargrove and

hugged Marla's legs. Marla patted her daughter's head.

"It's nice to see that Sammy likes Lester," Mrs. Hargrove said from her place at Marla's side. "Look at them talking away."

Sammy and Les *were* talking. And gesturing. And Marla suddenly remembered why Sammy had been back here, anyway. He'd been going to get that plastic shepherd he'd stolen from the church.

"Well, look at that," a man's voice said behind Mrs. Hargrove. "Over there at the end of the woodpile."

Marla didn't know how many ends a woodpile could have, but it didn't take more than one good look in the general direction of where the wood had been to see what the older man was talking about.

"There's our shepherd," Elmer said triumphantly, and then he paused. "Or what's left of him, anyway."

The shepherd looked as if he had been hit by a rock slide, which, Marla supposed, he almost had been. The plastic staff in his arm had been broken off and a log had dented his face. She couldn't tell from where she stood, but it looked as if some of the brown on his beard had been scraped off. He probably had more damage in the part she couldn't see.

"Well, what's the shepherd doing back here?" Charley asked as he stepped forward until he was even with Mrs. Hargrove.

"I don't think that's important now," Mrs. Hargrove said softly.

"Well, it didn't walk over here," Elmer said as he, too, stepped forward. "I wonder if Les brought it over."

Marla watched as the deputy sheriff and Sammy started walking over to them. Les had his hand on Sammy's shoulder and her son looked okay with it. Except for this morning, Sammy had been shrugging off her hand when she tried to guide him in that manner, even though he used to let his father steer him that way all the time. Marla had thought it was just something Sammy didn't like, since he was a little older. Now she realized it was just her hand he didn't want.

"Well, when would Les have time to do that?" Charley turned around and asked. "He came right over here from the café."

Marla looked away from her son and back to those near her. She could tell the instant Charley understood what it meant that Les had come here after the café. When no one had been surprised at seeing the shepherd away from the rest of the Nativity set, she realized that the deputy sheriff was not the only one in Dry Creek who had known that the plastic figure was missing.

"Well, no harm done," Charley murmured, half to himself.

"But—" Elmer started to ask, and then stopped when he saw the look on Charley's face.

"No harm done," Charley repeated as he stepped back to stand beside Mrs. Hargrove. "Those sheep aren't real, anyway, so they don't need a shepherd."

"Maybe the angel can watch them," Becky said. "They're just babies."

"Yeah," Charley agreed. "They're just babies."

"It's good to take care of the young ones," Elmer added.

Marla knew what the older people were trying to do. And it was nice of them. But she also knew what that kind of pity turned to and she knew that, given some time to think about it, all three of those older people would begin to look down on her family. It was just the way of it. They would think she wasn't raising her children right or that the children were just naturally bad or something.

"Sammy took the shepherd," Marla said. She might as well get that part of it out there. She wouldn't tell them her son was halfway to being a gang member, but she could face them knowing about the shepherd. "He—he—well, it's been a hard year. We'll pay to have it fixed, of course. Or to buy a new one."

Les and Sammy arrived just as Marla spoke again. "Of course, we should buy a new one. Just let me know where to buy it."

"There's no need to do that," Mrs. Hargrove protested. "The church can take care of it."

"Besides, the women sent away for the set," Charley said. "I don't think you can get it without the soup-can labels and I'm not sure how much more soup we can eat around here."

"Sammy's already promised to fix it," Les said. "We've got it all arranged."

"I don't know," Elmer said. "Did you see the hole in the shepherd's head?"

Les nodded. "I think we can fix it."

"We can pay you for your time," Marla offered. She didn't know where she was going to get all this money, but she did not want to be indebted to anyone in this small town.

"Sammy's going to help me with some

chores," Les said. "We've got a deal. I help him—he helps me."

Now, why did that make her feel so left out? Marla wondered. She should be grateful a man was taking some interest in Sammy. "Thank you."

"And, of course, he's also helping the church," Les said with a smile for Mrs. Hargrove. "Meet your new Sunday-school helper."

"Oh, my," Mrs. Hargrove said with a smile. "That's wonderful. I need someone to help me get the class ready for the Christmas program."

Marla wished she could tell what people were really thinking. Mrs. Hargrove was acting as if everything was just the way it was supposed to be. Marla couldn't believe, though, that the woman didn't have any feelings about having a young thief assigned to help her with her Sunday-school class. Marla would rather people just showed their horror and got it over with. That way she wouldn't have to wait for the day when they made it clear that, as charitable as they had been to the poor family when they so desperately needed help, they didn't really consider the Gossett family on the same level as everyone else in their town.

Marla knew all about the price one paid for

charity. She just hoped she could spare her children that knowledge.

"Sammy isn't used to church," Marla said to Mrs. Hargrove.

"I don't much like glitter," Sammy added. "On my wings. If I have to be an angel."

Maybe it was his near fall, but Marla noticed Sammy didn't look as upset about his wings as he had earlier.

"Well, maybe we'll think of something else to put on your wings," Mrs. Hargrove said as she stepped close to Sammy. "Why don't we go back to the café and talk about it? You and your sister never did get your orange juice."

Marla decided it was too late to hold on to her family's pride and she answered Mrs. Hargrove's look with a nod. "Thank you. I think I'll stay here for a minute, if that's okay."

Mrs. Hargrove nodded. "You don't have to worry about the kids when they're with me."

"Tell Linda I'll pay for their juices when I get there."

"I've never met anyone so determined to pay for everything," Les said.

Marla hadn't noticed that he'd walked closer to her. Maybe that's because all she could see was that Sammy was walking beside Mrs. Hargrove and she had her hand on his shoulder and he was actually smiling up at her. Marla knew Sammy certainly never smiled at *her* when she tried to put her hand on his shoulder. Not the way he did with Les and Mrs. Hargrove.

"My son hates me," Marla said before she remembered that the deputy sheriff was practically a stranger to her. Sure, he'd just helped her with her son, but he was doing that because he was on duty. She forced herself to smile up at him. "I guess all sons have problems with their mothers."

Les grunted. "He doesn't *hate* you. He was scared. Maybe even a little embarrassed."

Marla nodded. She wasn't about to bare her soul to someone she hardly knew. "I never realized the woodpile was such a danger to the kids."

Les relaxed. For a minute there, he'd thought Marla was going to fall apart. Nothing made him more nervous than a woman who looked as if she was going to lose control of her emotions. He'd been mistaken, though. She was just feeling the normal guilt that any parent would feel when they had not foreseen a danger that one of their children faced.

He'd watched her eyes lighten as she talked. Her face was still pale from the cold and her eyes were damp as if she'd cried a bit. It was funny that her tears didn't bother him. The thought of her crying made him want to move closer to her, not flee.

"The wood will be fine now that it's not in that pile," Les said. He couldn't just stand there and stare at her. She'd think he was having a shock reaction to what had happened, and he didn't want to worry her. "I'm surprised old man Gossett didn't have a wood chute on the back porch. Usually people have a rack like that to keep a good supply of logs inside where it's dry. Then there's not so much danger of the woodpile falling."

"We don't have anything like that," Marla said.

Les noticed how her hair curled around the wool scarf she had around her neck.

"I could make you a chute," Les offered.

"Oh, I couldn't ask you to do that."

"It's no problem."

"Well, I'll pay you."

Les shook his head. "Nobody needs to be paying anybody."

He wondered what made this woman so determined to pay for any friendly gesture anyone made toward her. He considered it a small mercy that she didn't keep protesting when he refused her payment this time.

She looked up at him. "I can never repay you, anyway. Not after you saved my son's life."

Ah, here come the tears, Les thought. He was glad it was just the two of them. He wouldn't want to be seen comforting Marla in the middle of the street in Dry Creek. He would have a dozen people watching and speculating on when he'd be proposing to her. But back here, behind the house—well, he wouldn't mind if she needed a shoulder to cry on.

"I suppose it's just all in a day's work for you, though," Marla said as she blinked away the tears in her eyes.

"What?" Les snapped back to reality. Gone was the warm, golden picture of Marla turning to him for comfort. She didn't even see him as anything more than a public servant out to do his duty.

"Well, I suppose it's not every day that you rescue someone from a woodpile," Marla continued with a bright smile. "I'd guess it's mostly drug problems, isn't it?"

"Whatever gave you that idea?"

"Your morning foot patrol. I figure you're out looking for drug dealers."

Les shook his head. "It's more a stray-cat patrol than anything at that hour."

"Oh. Well, that's good, then. What kind of crime *do* you have in Dry Creek?"

Les had never thought he'd be sitting on an old log behind a girl's house at his age. And if he had pictured himself doing something like that, he'd certainly never expected to be spending the time telling her about the crime life in Dry Creek. And even if he'd seen all those other things coming, he would never, ever have expected to be enjoying it so much. He liked watching her eyes while he told her stories.

Chapter Six

Marla didn't know why the deputy sheriff didn't just put handcuffs on Sammy and escort him into church. Or brand his forehead with a *T* for thief. She had expected Les to check to be sure that Sammy showed up in Mrs. Hargrove's Sunday-school class, but she hadn't expected him to wait for them in front of the church.

Les wasn't even standing on the porch or near the Nativity set like the other church people. There was no mistaking his interest for being social rather than business. He was pacing back and forth on the edge of the street, clearly waiting for them. He looked so official everyone must notice it. Especially because, Marla saw as she got closer to him, he was wearing his khaki sheriff's uniform.

She'd never even seen Les in a uniform until

now. He never wore a uniform when he walked around Dry Creek. That alone should tell people he was working. It certainly made a statement to her.

Marla kept her back straight. She didn't want people to think she was bothered at being on the business end of a sheriff's concern. After all, Sammy was making amends. They had nothing to be ashamed of.

"He's not in a suit," Sammy muttered. He was walking on one side of Marla and Becky was on the other. "And he's the sheriff."

"He's got his uniform on. And he's the temporary sheriff," Marla said. She didn't know why that made a difference to her, but it did. It meant that someday when Les Wilkerson passed her on the streets of Dry Creek he wouldn't be obliged to greet her just because he had her son in some kind of casual probation situation. He wouldn't need to be an official keeper of her son's schedule. He'd be able to choose whether or not he wanted to be their friend. He might even change out of his uniform when he planned to meet her.

"He's wearing boots. Why can't I get boots?" Sammy continued.

Marla took note of Sammy's comment with hope. His *amigos* didn't wear cowboy boots. Of

course, they didn't wear suits, either, and that
was Sammy's biggest complaint this morning.

Not that she blamed him about the suit. She
could blame him for other things, but not for
that. She'd bought both of their suits at a dis-
count store in the garment district of down-
town Los Angeles so they'd have something
appropriate to wear for Jorge's funeral. And
she hated the black suit she had on even more
than Sammy disliked his suit.

After Jorge's funeral she'd vowed never to
wear her suit again. The thing made her look
like a crow. She'd noticed that fact when she
looked in the mirror after the funeral. It was
the worst day of her life, and all she could do
was think of the crows in the cemetery where
they had buried Jorge. She'd been struck at the
time how much her black suit made her look
like them, all squawky and ugly and sitting on
lone branches in those trees, each one spread
out so they were all by themselves looking
fierce and protective of their aloneness.

The suit didn't just make her look like a
crow, it made her feel like one, too.

She had almost given the suit to the Salva-
tion Army before she moved up to Dry Creek,
and now she wished she had. The only other
thing resembling a dress she even had in her

closet was a south-of-the-border senorita skirt-and-blouse set. She couldn't wear that to church here, though, so if she hadn't had the black suit, she could truthfully have told herself she had nothing to wear and maybe she could have justified staying home. Instead, she was left with trying to make that suit look better with a coffee-colored tank top and a black pearl necklace. She'd even found a gold circle brooch to wear on the lapel.

She wasn't sure any of it softened the suit enough, and she had finally given up. Maybe if she went for the grim look, people would stare at her instead of spending so much time studying Sammy, anyway.

"You're here," Les said when Marla and her children came within speaking distance.

Marla nodded with a quick look at the assortment of people gathered at the steps leading into the church. "We said we'd be here. It's our agreement."

Not for the first time, she wished Sammy hadn't stolen something from a church. Of course, she wished mostly that he had never stolen anything from anywhere, but if he had to steal, why a church? She'd rather have to volunteer for a school function or even put in some hours at the local hardware store. But a church? She didn't know anything about churches. The truth was they scared her a little bit.

She'd certainly never expected to have a sheriff's escort when she entered the church in Dry Creek for the first time.

Everyone was watching her and the kids as they walked up to the steps leading into the building. She wondered if she had "visitor" stamped on her forehead. If she did, it probably said "official visitor—sentence being served."

"Welcome," a man said, dipping his hat to her as she walked past.

"Good to see you here," another added with a smile.

Fortunately, Les reached Marla's side about then and he ushered her through the rest of the people standing on the church steps. Marla didn't know what she would say to any of them if they asked her if she knew what had happened to the missing shepherd. Of course, they might not even need to ask the question if they thought about Les escorting them into the church in full uniform.

Marla didn't know how a man could be so self-contained. Les didn't look as if he was doing his duty this morning, but he didn't look relaxed, either. He nodded to various people, but he had his hand on her elbow and he was guiding her up the stairs.

Marla would have paid good money to know what was going on in that head of his. He'd cut his hair since she'd seen him earlier in the week. And he was wearing some cologne that smelled good. He gave everyone a smooth smile, but his eyes looked a little anxious. She hoped he wasn't worried that Sammy would back out of his agreement. Sammy had his problems, it was true, but he didn't go back on his word. At least, she didn't think he did.

Marla sighed. She needed to face the fact that she didn't know her son very well anymore.

Les wondered for the first time if it was such a good thing to have suggested some service to the church as a way for Sammy to make amends for taking the shepherd. Marla and the kids all looked as if they were facing a judge. Or an executioner. He'd liked the way Marla looked in the bathrobe better than he did in this suit of hers. Maybe the suit material was scratchy and that's why she held herself so stiffly. She might have been annoyed with him when she answered her door in her bathrobe the other morning, but she'd looked happier then than she did now.

"Mrs. Hargrove will tell you how to do everything," Les said to Sammy as he motioned for the boy to continue up the walk ahead of him. "You might even surprise yourself and have fun."

"He's not supposed to have fun," Marla said as she stepped closer so only Les could hear her words. "He's supposed to learn a lesson."

"Well, it doesn't need to be painful. Mrs. Hargrove likes to keep things happy in her class. There's lots of singing and stories."

"So I could take my suit jacket off?" Sammy asked as he looked up at Les. "I don't want to scare any little kids."

"You'll wear the suit jacket," Marla said.

Les lifted his hands in surrender. "Your mom's the one with the say here."

"Nobody wears a suit," Sammy mumbled. "It's lame."

Les shrugged. "They say it makes you look older."

Sammy looked up at him skeptically. "Old enough to be *dead* maybe."

"I'm just repeating what the girls say."

"Then why don't you have a suit on?"

Les wondered suddenly if he should have a

suit on. Marla was wearing a suit. Her son was wearing a suit. Maybe she expected everyone to be wearing suits. That's probably the way it was in Los Angeles. Suddenly he was unsure of himself. He'd put on his uniform because it was the most dressy thing he owned. But maybe it had been a mistake.

"Don't talk that way to the sheriff," Marla scolded Sammy quietly. "It's none of our business how he's dressed."

Les looked down at his khaki slacks. They were clean. And pressed. He even wore his regulation dark tie with his uniform shirt. He looked at the other men who stood around the Nativity set. No one there was wearing a suit or a uniform. Of course, Pastor Matthew would wear a suit. But he would probably be the only man in the church building wearing one. Unless anyone counted Sammy. Les had a spurt of empathy for the boy.

"Hey, what happened to the shepherd?" one of the ranch hands from the Elkton place called over to Les when he was at the top of the stairs. "He was the only figure in the whole Nativity set that I can relate to and he isn't here."

Several ranch hands were standing around the Nativity set admiring it. Les could see where one of them had brought in a bale of straw to scatter around the manger. Mary was surrounded by the stuff.

"The shepherd got a bit damaged," Les said. He was speaking, but people were looking at the space where the shepherd had been. He was grateful to have the attention off himself. "Don't worry, though. We're fixing him up. He'll be better than new before you know it."

"That angel needs to be rehung," another ranch hand said. "She's going to fall if we don't do something."

Les nodded. Sammy had called it right. "Maybe we can get a ladder from the hardware store after church and restring her."

Marla had been holding her breath when Les was talking to the men. She was surprised the other men didn't ask more questions about how the shepherd had been damaged. But they seemed to trust that Les was taking care of whatever was wrong. She hoped the rest of the people in the church were as easily satisfied about the shepherd.

Someone rang a bell and suddenly everyone was walking up the steps into the church. Marla was grateful that Les hung back and walked with her and the children instead of going ahead with the other men.

Marla relaxed as soon as she walked into the church. There, at the front, was a large wooden cross. It reminded her of the one she had at home. It was made of the same hard polished wood. She wondered if the people here knew what Jorge had discovered by looking at his cross in his dying days.

The air smelled of pine—someone had placed a big Christmas tree in front of the church, off to the left side. There was a piano on the right side and a young blonde woman sat at it playing a Christmas hymn. The notes sounded full and smooth.

"The adults have a class up here," Les said. He seemed to be nodding a greeting to a dozen people while he talked to her. "Mrs. Hargrove will take Sammy and Becky down to her class."

"But shouldn't I be with them?"

"Ma," Sammy protested. "You don't need to come."

"They'll be fine with Mrs. Hargrove. And don't worry about Becky. Mrs. Hargrove already suggested she might like her class better than the one for the younger kids, especially if Sammy is there. Here comes Mrs. Hargrove now."

Marla knew the children would be okay with

the older woman. She was just so used to having them with her. She wondered if she would be okay without them.

Mrs. Hargrove greeted everyone and pointed the children in the direction of a doorway before Marla finished wondering what she should do. She relaxed when even Becky seemed unconcerned that Marla wasn't going with them. Her children were growing up.

"The kids' classes are in the basement," Les said as he nodded to the nearest row of pews. "The adults sit up here in comfort."

The pews were the same smooth wood as the cross, but Marla wasn't sure she would be comfortable even if the pews had deep cushions. As a child, church people had given her family charity baskets, but they had never invited them to come to their churches. If Marla had to be in a church at all, she would like to be in the back row so she could duck out if she discovered she wasn't welcome.

Unfortunately, Les wasn't gesturing toward the back row. And so Marla reluctantly walked with him to the front pew.

"I'm not used to churches," Marla said quietly as Les waited for her to enter the aisle space before him. "They make me a little nervous that I'll do something out of place."

"Don't worry. You can't make any mistakes," Les said as she sat on the pew and he joined her.

"I brought something for the offering plate. It's not much, but—"

"You don't need to put anything in the plate."

"I can afford to give something to the church."

Marla wondered how everyone could be so relaxed and friendly to everyone else. She'd already been given more welcoming smiles than she'd ever seen in Los Angeles. In ways the small town of Dry Creek reminded her of the town in Mexico where her mother had grown up. Marla had spent a couple of weeks with one of her aunts there when she was a teenager. People had the same unconscious interest in a stranger there as they did in Dry Creek. In Los Angeles, no one looked at strangers. Here, everyone looked her in the eye and greeted her.

"Surely some of them know about Sammy and the shepherd," Marla said, her voice low so only Les could hear.

"I doubt it. Mrs. Hargrove can keep a secret, and she'll see that Charley and Elmer watch their tongues, too."

Marla relaxed. Maybe things would work out for them in Dry Creek, after all. Maybe she was worrying too much. Maybe people were more tolerant here than she expected.

The pastor stood up then and walked to the front of the pews, opening his Bible on the way.

Marla had never heard the story of the young Mary before. Oh, she knew all about the baby Jesus being born in a manger and the angel proclaiming the good news to the shepherds. Anyone who received Christmas cards knew that much. But she had never heard anyone talk about how Mary must have felt when she was pregnant and had to ride that donkey off into a new land just to satisfy some bureaucrat someplace.

Marla had never expected to feel kinship with someone in the Bible. She thought all those people had lived golden lives where they floated on clouds and lived the special sweat-free lives of saints. She had never imagined Mary would possibly have had morning sickness. Or felt fat, just as Marla had felt during both her pregnancies.

As the pastor spoke, Marla got a vivid picture of how awkward everything must have been for Mary. There was no hot water in the manger. Not even a bed to lie down on. Marla knew firsthand how it felt to not even have basic furniture. And to be a woman in a strange land. She knew about that, too.

Marla might not be pregnant right now, but she, like Mary, knew the uncertainty that children brought to a woman's life. She didn't know for sure what to do with Sammy. He didn't seem to want her sympathy and support. Marla really identified with Mary, though, when she realized that Mary had also needed to trust a man with her deepest secret.

Marla looked over at Les when the pastor talked about how vulnerable Mary must have felt, knowing Joseph could judge her harshly. He not only knew her secret; he also controlled her future.

Les wouldn't be a bad person to trust, Marla supposed. Although she couldn't help but notice he was scowling at the man who had sat down on the other side of her. This was the same man who had greeted her outside at the Nativity set, and he seemed harmless enough. There, the man smiled at her again. She could see Les's scowl out of the corner of her eye. She wondered if Joseph had spent the trip to Bethlehem scowling, too. No wonder Mary always seemed so quiet in those pageants.

The adults' class ended with a prayer for peace in Dry Creek and throughout the rest of the world. Marla looked around to see if anyone focused on the cross at the front of the church when they prayed, but it seemed as if everyone just closed their eyes. Someday when she knew everyone better she was going to have to ask someone about the purpose of the cross in prayer. The cross looked too important to be a decoration, but she hadn't seen anyone do anything with it. Of course, she didn't want to ask any questions now that would reveal her ignorance.

After the prayer, Les suggested that they have some coffee in the kitchen area. He looked as if he had something to say, but somehow no words ever came out, so Marla just followed him. She counted herself lucky that she didn't have to ride a donkey along the way.

Les wondered how he could have forgotten the ranch hands. He should have known they would all be at church when word got out that a new single female was going to be there. Most of them came, anyway, during the Christmas season, so an eligible woman was just an added bonus.

"That man has worked at the Elkton place for almost ten years now," Les finally said as he nodded toward Byron and then led Marla back to the table where the coffee was being served. He didn't want to criticize Byron, but he hoped Marla would realize a man who only worked on a ranch wasn't as ambitious as a man who actually owned his own ranch.

"That must be nice," Marla said.

Les looked at her. How could it be nice?

"To work in the same place for that long."

"Yeah, well." He barely restrained himself from mentioning that he had worked in the same place for almost twice as long and it was his own place.

Les noticed that Byron was walking back to the coffee table just as they were. The ranch hand didn't have a suit on, but Les could plainly see that the man's shirt and pants went together as if they belonged in a magazine ad somewhere. Of course, Les's shirt and pants matched, as well, but khaki and khaki didn't exactly make a man stand out from the pack.

Les felt a frown settling on his face. Byron was dressed like a man who charmed women, and Les knew the ranch hand could do it. Byron had even talked himself out of eating soup during the drive for labels and the women he'd charmed to do that were safely married, so they didn't even have anything to gain by giving in to his smiles. Les calculated every man in Dry Creek had had to eat ten extra cans of soup to make up for Byron's share.

Les knew that women didn't judge men by the same scales other men used, however. Marla probably liked a man like Byron, Les thought as his frown deepened.

Les had just decided to stop thinking about the man when Byron planted himself squarely in their path. Les still had his hand on Marla's arm and he felt his grip tighten slightly. She was, technically, his guest and he wasn't giving her up to Byron. Still, he supposed he needed to be civil. "Do you mind if we pass? We're going for coffee."

Byron turned with a grin. "Thanks. Don't mind if I do join you. I heard Mrs. Hargrove made cowboy coffee this morning."

Les knew he had lost the battle before Byron even turned his attention to Marla.

"I don't think I've had the pleasure of meeting you," Byron said to Marla with that smile of his.

Les saw Marla turn a little pink. He could tell by the slight sparkle in her eyes that Byron's smile was not wasted on her. Of course, how could she know that Byron had perfected that smile in front of a mirror? At least, that was the rumor when Les had known him in high school.

"This is Marla Gossett," Les said. What else could he do? "Marla, meet Byron Stead."

Marla nodded as she looked at Byron. "What's cowboy coffee?"

"Good enough for a cowboy and strong enough for his horse, too."

Les almost shook his head. How did the man make it sound as if he'd invented something wonderful? Mrs. Hargrove had made the same coffee she made every Sunday and it had nothing to do with cowboys or horses. Byron had a way with words, all right. Les was just waiting for him to make some reference to the poet Lord Byron. The man had been named after the poet, but Les knew full well that it didn't mean Byron had any real writing talent. In fact, if his high school record still held, he couldn't even spell.

Of course, Les supposed it wasn't spelling that put those sparkles in women's eyes. Still, any self-respecting ranch hand would change his name to Brian, no matter what nonsense his mother had been thinking when he was born.

"There's cinnamon orange tea this morning, too," Les said to Marla as the three of them reached the coffee table. "They always have it out around Christmas."

"I'll get you a cup of the tea unless—" Byron started.

"I can get it," Les interrupted. He was the host.

Byron looked at him in surprise, and Les supposed he couldn't blame him. Les had never competed with the ranch hands for a woman's attention before. Les had always thought a woman who was taken in by the likes of someone like Byron wasn't the woman for him, anyway. Unfortunately, that included most women. He wasn't going to risk that it included Marla.

"I was going to say—unless you want to try the coffee," Byron continued with a smile for Marla.

Les watched Byron move his shoulder slightly to make it seem as though Marla was with him and not with Les. Before Les could step forward to block Byron, Marla stepped forward herself.

"Shouldn't I be checking on the children?" she said with a look at Les.

Les nodded, even though no one ever needed to check on their children in Sunday school here. "It wouldn't hurt."

Les had never been prouder than when he was walking Marla to the steps that led to the downstairs classrooms. He knew he was a quiet man; he liked it that way. But it did feel good to have a woman choose to walk off with him in that quietness instead of drinking tea with Byron.

"Does Sammy have to put in a certain number of hours?" Marla asked as she started down the stairs.

Les felt his pride leave him. He'd forgotten there for a minute that Marla was walking with him because he was the deputy sheriff and she was worried about her son. "No, there's no set hours."

Marla nodded. "I'm sure the time he spends with Mrs. Hargrove will only help him." Then she looked up. "And with you, too. I can't thank you enough for helping him."

"It's no problem."

Les's only consolation was that Marla had already agreed to bring Sammy out to his ranch tomorrow so they could begin work on repairing the shepherd. Once he had her out there, he wouldn't need to worry about any other single ranch hands. Mr. Morales was supposed to drop by tomorrow morning, but he was old enough to be Marla's father.

Les could see the part in Marla's hair as he followed her down the stairs. Her hair fell straight on both sides of the part and he liked the way it swayed as she walked. He thought with a start that it looked like Mrs. Hargrove's coffee when it was being poured into one of the larger church mugs. Which, now that he thought about it, wasn't a half-bad piece of poetic nonsense for a rancher to come up with.

He silently thought the words. *Your hair is like coffee, pouring straight...to—straight to—*

Well, Les told himself, he'd finish the words later. It was the thought that counted. Women liked poems about their hair. Byron, the poet, would never have found the words to an image like that, Les told himself with satisfaction. Maybe he'd put some sparkles in Marla's eyes yet.

Chapter Seven

Marla drove her car down the long gravel road, wondering if the metal sign she'd seen earlier indicating that this was the Wilkerson ranch was accurate. If it was, Les's place was huge. A fence ran along one side of the road, and on the other side, hills covered with dead brown grass stretched all the way to the distant mountains. Snow lay here and there, especially in the ravines, and the ground still glistened from last night's frost.

Fortunately, the road was clear. Two tire ruts showed the way. She had driven over a cattle guard in the road as she entered the ranch, but she had not seen any animals yet. They must be tucked away in some of those snowy ravines.

Marla looked over and saw Sammy staring out the side window. Becky was in the backseat.

"Big, isn't it?" Marla asked. The only other time she had visited a ranch like this was in Mexico, where one of her uncles worked. He'd driven her around and told her about things like cattle guards and ravines and drought.

Sammy grunted. "I don't see those sheep he was talking about."

"The babies?" Becky asked from the backseat.

"If they're young, they probably need to be near the barn."

That was Marla's best guess. Her uncle had never taken her to the ranch's buildings, and she'd never had pets to care for. But the young ones probably always needed special care no matter what species they were. And a barn was an awful lot like the stable where Mary had stayed when she had the baby Jesus, so Marla figured the babies would always be there.

"Maybe we'll see the little lambs," Becky said.

"Maybe."

It was Monday and Marla was bringing Sammy out to the sheriff's place so that they could start fixing the Nativity shepherd. Correction, she told herself. They were going to

Les's place. He had asked her to call him Les, and she'd done pretty well at church yesterday until she'd thought of him in his law enforcement role. Somehow it didn't seem right to call him by his first name when his duty required him to discipline her son. Still, she would try to honor the man's request when she saw him today.

She wondered if Les had unloaded the plastic shepherd. He had put it into the back of his pickup last week and he'd driven a late-model car to church, so she hadn't seen the pickup since. She supposed he wouldn't have been able to leave the plastic figure in his pickup if he had to use the vehicle for chores, but she had hoped Sammy would be there to help him carry the figure inside to where they were going to work on it.

She wanted Sammy to see every ounce of effort that was going into righting his wrong.

They should be reaching Les's house soon, Marla thought as she started up a slight incline. She looked at the clock on her dashboard and saw that she was right on schedule. He'd suggested they come for a nine-o'clock breakfast, and it was ten minutes to the hour. It would take her a few minutes to get the car parked and the kids' jackets zipped up again before leaving the car and then going to Les's door.

Marla hadn't told the children that a real shepherd might be there this morning, as well. From the man's name, Mr. Morales, Marla suspected he was Hispanic. She almost hoped so. She didn't want to hide her Hispanic background any longer, and with another Hispanic there, it would be natural to mention that she and the children were of the same heritage.

Les had seemed pretty easygoing so far. She'd just have to trust him to accept their Hispanic roots without letting his mind wander to any thoughts of big-city gangs. Up here, she doubted anyone had even heard of the 19th Street gang. Maybe she was worrying for nothing. She knew Sammy had used the gang symbol on his note, but no one seemed to be asking what it all meant. Of course, she knew why he'd written it. He had been missing his *amigos* in Los Angeles. But missing his old friends wasn't a crime no matter how unsuitable those friends were.

Les looked out the kitchen window for the hundredth time that morning. He could see the road coming up to his house through this window, so it was the only window worth looking out when he was expecting someone.

The house and barn had already been here when he'd bought the ranch land, or he would have built them on one of the higher pieces of ground. Fortunately, it never flooded this far from Big Dry Creek, so the lower elevation wasn't a problem. And the dip in the land did help with the wind. Being stuck down in this bowl made it hard to know when company was coming, though, and Les liked to be prepared when people drove up to his place.

Not that he could stand preparing any more than he had this morning.

He had been up since five o'clock trying to get everything ready for Marla and the kids, and he hadn't done anything for the past hour except pace from the kitchen window to the living room. Back and forth. He went over his mental checklist.

He'd scoured down the kitchen and swept out the barn yesterday after church. He usually kept Sunday as a day of rest, but he figured the Lord knew how he felt about company coming. At first it was going to be only a little bit of cleaning. The barn was a big old building, and Les was proud of the restoring he'd done to it. He'd replaced most of the stalls and added a workshop space with an electric heater. He hadn't had a chance to work on the old hayloft, though, and he'd have to remember to caution everyone not to go up there. All in all, he was proud of the barn, and it always looked good when it had been swept clean of hay.

After he'd finished in the barn, he'd brought the plants in from the porch and set them here and there around the living room. He'd place a plant on the bookcase and then notice that the coffee table looked a little beat-up, so he'd move the plant there until he noticed that the windowsill looked naked with nothing on it. That's what he'd been doing earlier this morning.

Finally Les had faced the fact that there was nothing else he could do. Marla and the kids would either like his home or they wouldn't. Somehow, the starkness of that realization wasn't as comforting as he'd thought it would be. He looked around for something more to do. He was beginning to see why women in the old days had doilies to arrange on their furniture. It gave them something to do before company was coming.

When Les had finished positioning the plants for the third time that morning, he'd decided he better start to make the scones. He'd gotten the recipe from a website on his computer the day he'd brought the damaged shepherd figure back here. Even then he knew he'd want to give Marla and the kids something to eat when they came out, and the scones looked simple enough to make.

Les's mother used to make scones when she had women friends come over, so he decided they were the thing to make for Marla.

Les believed a man could do anything with a computer behind him. He'd used his computer to design a bridge over the creek that flowed through his north pasture. He'd calculated the amount of feed he needed to raise a calf to be a yearling. He had absolute faith that a computer could help him make scones.

Last night Les had left the scone directions on the kitchen counter next to a bowl. Any kind of baked goods tasted best if they were fresh from the oven, so he didn't want to bake them Sunday evening.

Not all men would know that fact, Les told himself. A smart woman would recognize the benefits of marrying a man who had done his own cooking for years. Not that it was time to be talking about marriage with Marla. He'd be happy if he could get her to go out on a date with him. And kiss him. A kiss would be a good thing. Maybe if he worked in the poem about her hair, she'd start thinking of him as someone she'd like to kiss.

The scones were barely in the oven when Les started to worry that he'd forgotten to latch the gate on the lamb pen. He knew he never forgot to close any gates completely, but he kept trying to remember if he'd heard the click of that particular gate. If it didn't click, a lamb could nudge it open if he tried hard enough.

Finally Les decided he should go check. It wouldn't look good if Marla came over the hill and the lambs were running all over the place. She would think he couldn't take care of things. No woman wanted to kiss a man who couldn't take care of things.

Les put on his winter coat and stomped back out to the barn.

The gate was latched, but one of the lambs was standing just inside it looking rather forlorn, so Les took a minute to give him some help back to his mother. By the time Les got back into the house, the scones had burned a little. The burn was more of a dark brown than a black and, ordinarily, Les would have pronounced them good enough to eat.

But he didn't want to serve burned scones to Marla, so he made a batch of biscuits. Fortunately, he could make biscuits in his sleep. He had a jar of homemade rhubarb jam that Mrs. Hargrove had given him for Christmas last year. He'd been saving it for special company, and today was about as special as it was likely to get.

Les felt as if he'd thrown hay bales all day by the time he saw the car coming up his driveway.

Then he remembered he wanted to have classical music playing when Marla drove up, so he quickly went to the stereo in his living room and turned it on. He wanted her to know that a rancher could be cultured. He wasn't putting his complete faith in his biscuits, even though Mrs. Hargrove had once pronounced them the lightest ones she'd ever eaten.

Unfortunately, Les had forgotten about the plant he'd just placed on top of the shelf above the stereo. The one that hadn't looked quite right on the coffee table. He'd been so sure the philodendron would balance out the room with its vine of leaves that trailed down to the stereo itself. Les had to lean forward to find the CD he wanted to play. He heard footsteps on the porch at the same instant he saw the pot above him begin to tip.

* * *

Marla heard a faint crash. She had her hand all ready to knock on the kitchen door, but when she heard the crash, she froze.

"Something fell," Sammy said.

"I'm sure Deputy Wilker—I mean, Les—has it all under control."

It hadn't sounded like a person falling, so Marla figured Les was all right.

"Maybe he dropped the shepherd again," Becky said.

"Sammy, don't—" Marla started, but it was too late. Sammy was already leaning over and looking in the window at the side of the kitchen door.

"Ah, he's all right," Sammy said as he straightened.

Les opened the door.

Marla started to smile. The man had a leaf in his ear. And a trail of dirt on his shirt.

"I hope you like Beethoven," Les said as he stood there looking a little uncertain.

Marla nodded, and then she heard music fill the house. There must be speakers in every room. "It's lovely."

Les relaxed. "I can do Bach instead, if you'd rather."

"I like them both."

Marla was surprised to remember how much she liked classical music. Jorge hadn't liked it, calling it funeral music, so she'd turned the car radio away from the classical station years ago. She hadn't turned it back, but she promised herself she would. She had no one to please anymore but herself, and it felt good.

"Come in and have a seat at the table while I go change."

Marla tried not to be too envious as she looked around the kitchen. Les had gone into another room and, for once, her children were quietly sitting, waiting for him to come back and serve them the biscuits he'd promised. She would have to remember that the smell of baked biscuits was enough to make her children behave.

Their silence left Marla time to look around. What a kitchen this was. She wished her mother was alive to see it.

When had a kitchen like this become an impossible dream for her? It wasn't even the appliances that she envied, although they were all better than the ones she'd ever had. It was the space. Her mother always said she wanted a kitchen big enough for dancing, and Marla had understood why when she had seen one of her uncles dance with his wife in their kitchen one day in Mexico. A kitchen big enough to dance in would hold a table sturdy enough for children's games. A kitchen like that was meant for family life.

Her mother had never had a kitchen like that in her whole life.

The kitchen in Marla's house was cramped. It wasn't much bigger than the one in her old apartment, and that had been a galley kitchen with barely enough room for one person to move up and down the aisle from refrigerator to sink to stove.

When Les came back wearing a clean shirt, Marla flushed. She shouldn't be sitting here wishing she had this man's kitchen. "Can I help with anything?"

"Thanks, but it'll only take me a minute."

There were already place mats and plates on the table. Les got the biscuits and some butter before he sat down. Then he reached for the jar in the center of the table and popped its seal. Marla saw the homemade jam and forgot all about the appliances.

"Is that rhubarb? Don't tell me you made that?"

Les shook his head. "It's from Mrs. Hargrove."

"Good. I was going to start feeling intimidated if you knew how to make jam. I'm afraid my cooking is pretty plain."

"You make good tamales," Sammy said. "Remember, you said if you got a pork roast, you'd make the sweet ones for Christmas."

Marla caught her breath. She hadn't intended to tell Les about her heritage this soon in the day. She looked at him and didn't see anything new on his face. She turned to Sammy. "I don't have the pork roast yet. I've got it on my wish list, though. We'll have to see if they have a small one at the store."

"Now tamales, that's something I don't think I could ever make," Les said as he walked back to the refrigerator. "I make quesadillas once in a while, but that's as far as I go."

"Do you like Mexican food?" Marla asked. She supposed it didn't really matter one way or the other, but she was hoping to have at least one friend in Dry Creek and, she had to admit, it would be nice to have a friend who enjoyed her family's food and traditions. The deputy sheriff's acceptance of her and the kids mattered to her.

"Love it," Les said as he brought back a bowl of cut orange sections. "Just don't know how to make it."

"Oh." Marla smiled. She could take care of that part of it.

Les sat down and looked at Marla. "Do you mind if we say grace?"

"Of course not."

"Want to join hands?" Les held out his hands, one to Sammy and the other to Marla.

Marla wondered why she'd never thought to say grace with her children. Maybe if she'd spent some time talking to Sammy about God, her son would not have felt the need to idolize a bunch of criminals. Of course, to do that, she would have had to learn something about God herself. After her time in church yesterday, she thought she could do it, too. A God who had time for women like Mary might have time for her, too.

She was already learning more about prayer. For starters, there was something powerful about holding a man's hand in prayer. Marla let the feelings of security and abundance fill her. Everything seemed good when she bowed her head and held on to Les's hand as he prayed.

A few seconds later she was wondering how long people were supposed to hold hands. Les had finished praying and he'd let go of Sammy's hand, but he still held hers. Not that she was complaining exactly. It was just odd.

She'd opened her eyes when he said "Amen," and he'd looked over at her. She couldn't help but notice that his eyes were the color of moss. A friendly sort of moss with flecks in them. And his smile. He had a nice smile.

"I have a cross," she said to Les.

"Huh?"

He was still smiling. Only now he was rubbing the knuckle of her little finger.

"On my wall. The cross I have." She took a breath. "I know it's not like saying prayers and all of that. But…"

Marla supposed she should expect someone like Les to think she was a heathen. "It's just I've never known a man who prayed before— well, my uncles do, but I don't see them much."

"That's because they live in Mexico," Sammy said calmly. "Can I have a biscuit now?"

"It's not polite to ask," Marla said automatically.

Les flushed and let go of her hand. "Sure. Biscuits coming up for everyone."

"I can butter my own," Becky said as she lifted her knife to demonstrate.

"Just don't let her at the jam," Sammy said as he took a biscuit off the plate Les passed to him. "She'll get all sticky."

"I'll put the jam on for her," Marla said.

Marla had watched Les and she was beginning to wonder if the man was slow. Sammy had all but announced their heritage and Les hadn't reacted at all. Usually people at least had a question or two when someone told them about their roots. In fact, now that she thought about it for a moment, it was only polite to make some comment.

"My uncles live close to Puerto Vallarta," Marla said as she took the biscuit plate from Sammy. "My mother came from around there."

Les nodded as he split his biscuit and started to butter it. "My mother moved here from Boston. She had a hard time getting used to the casual way things are done around here. Not enough *sirs* and *ma'ams* to please her."

"But, at least the temperature would be about the same, wouldn't it?" Marla said politely. "Or is it colder here?"

Les grunted. "It's colder here than anywhere."

Marla was beginning to wonder if her coming from Mexico was the same to Les as his mother coming from Boston. She hoped it was. Since he hadn't made any comment, she would have to assume it was.

"It's warm in the state of Jalisco."

Les looked up.

"That's the area around Puerto Vallarta where my mother was born. There's lots of marine life. Tropical vegetation. Some shopping."

"Sounds great. I'd like to see it sometime."

"The police carry guns there," Sammy offered. "You should go and find out how they do it."

Les smiled. "Reserve deputy sheriffs don't need to carry guns."

"But you have one, right? If you needed it, you could get it?"

Her son looked a little anxious.

"Sammy!" Marla said. Why did young boys always want to know about guns? She wished Sammy never even thought about who carried a gun and who didn't. Fortunately, Sammy had never carried one, not even with his fascination with the 19th Street gang. She'd asked him that question directly and he'd told her no.

"That's all right," Les said to Marla, then he looked at Sammy. "No one should carry a gun just because they can. I have a rifle I keep in my pickup so I have it with me when I go up to the mountains. But that's the only time I might need it."

Sammy didn't seem particularly satisfied with Les's answer, but Marla shot him a warning glance. She didn't want Les to think that Sammy was overly interested in violence. Which he wasn't, of course. She still hadn't been able to ask herself if Sammy might have lied to her about whether or not he had handled a gun. But this kind of conversation could give Sammy a reputation as a troublemaker, whether he had ever done anything or not.

"That's the pickup you take when you come into Dry Creek?" Sammy pressed. "The one with the red stripe down the side."

"It's the only pickup I have."

Sammy nodded.

"I'm sure you keep your pickup locked," Marla said. She didn't want Sammy's curiosity to lead him into trouble.

"No one locks their pickups around here, but I keep the bullets with me, so the rifle isn't loaded, if that's what worries you."

Sammy didn't seem to react to that added piece of news, so Marla relaxed. Maybe she was being paranoid about Sammy's past. After all, that was behind them. He was in a new place now and none of his old friends could reach him here. There hadn't even been any more letters after that first one about the baseball he left behind. Her son was fine.

Before long breakfast was over and Les announced that it was time to go to the workshop in the barn. He assured them that Mr. Morales would come in around ten o'clock and help them with the shepherd's face.

"Is Mr. Morales Hispanic?" Marla asked.

Les shrugged. "I think so. I'm not sure where he comes from, though. He's never mentioned any family."

"Will he bring his sheep with him?" Becky asked.

"I'm afraid not." Les smiled at Becky. "But I have some lambs that have been wanting to meet a little girl."

"Like me?" Becky squealed.

Les nodded. "Just like you."

Les had extra scarves for the children to wrap around their necks and he helped Becky put her mittens on.

Marla noticed that the rancher was patient with her children. Those mittens weren't easy. He'd already shown that he would risk injury to himself to save her son from a bad situation. And he was helping Sammy make amends for breaking the shepherd, when many men would have just scolded him instead. Most men, she had noticed, would rather talk to a child than actually do something like put on a mitten or help a boy learn to repair something he'd broken.

If she was keeping score, Marla would have to admit that Les ranked high on the could-be-a-dad list. She was beginning to wonder why he was still single. He looked like the kind of guy women would marry in a heartbeat. He didn't have a handsome face. It was too weathered for that. But he had regular features and the nicest eyes. All of which probably meant he was single by choice.

Marla frowned as Les opened the door for all of them so they could go outside. Maybe he was single because he was so committed to the church. She wondered if Les was that kind of a religious man. That would certainly explain why he was kind to children and took such good care of his lambs and only kept a gun in his pickup instead of on his hip like most lawmen would do.

Marla's frown deepened. She never would have thought of Les as some type of kind, priestly uncle, but now that she was adding it all up, it made sense. She knew he didn't swagger around like some men, but he was strong enough for that if he had wanted to. Not many men could resist that temptation, especially when they'd just been a hero as Les had been the other day.

There was no getting around the fact that Les was unusual.

Well, she was glad she'd realized this early. She wasn't going to make the mistake of thinking he was interested in her in any romantic sense. She had a bad enough record just figuring out normal men like her late husband. She didn't need to start guessing about whether or not some saint loved her.

Chapter Eight

The barn was nicer than Marla had expected. It was cold outside, but she felt the heat the minute she stepped inside. There were hay bales lining one side and glass windows on the other. Several cows stood switching their tails in the sunshine that came in through the tall windows. Everything was neat and cozy. It made her feel good that Les kept such a warm, clean place for his animals, especially because in the spring most of the animals would probably be mothers and little babies.

Les pointed Marla and the kids toward the workshop room that he had made in one section of the barn.

"But what's up there?" Sammy asked before they reached the workshop.

Les looked up. "The hayloft. No one goes up there, though. It's not safe."

Marla could see where boards above her were sloping down. There were even a couple of places where a board had broken off and there was a hole in the ceiling of the lower part of the barn. There were thick beams holding the boards in place so they wouldn't be able to fall, though, so people were safe walking around below the loft. And Les had strung a rope across the wooden stairs at the side of the barn leading up to the hayloft to warn people not to climb the stairs.

Sammy shrugged as he stared up at the loft. "It looks okay. I've been in worse buildings."

There were some deserted buildings in Los Angeles and Marla was appalled to think that Sammy had actually been inside any of them. "That's why we came up here. You need to stay out of places like that."

"I should have fixed the hayloft last year."

"Oh, I didn't mean your place. You don't have to fix anything for us."

"I just didn't think I'd have company out here in the barn."

"We're not exactly company. You're doing us a favor by helping with the shepherd."

"I'm happy to do it. It's not a favor."

"Well, it's certainly a kindness."

Les opened his mouth, then closed it again. "Well, thank you."

Marla nodded. She was glad to have that settled.

Marla noticed that both Sammy and Becky had been watching her and Les.

"You don't have to worry about me. I won't go up there," Becky announced a little primly. "I just want to see the lambs."

"You're a good girl," Les muttered.

Sammy grunted. "That's because she still thinks Santa is watching."

Marla flushed. She didn't want to discuss their lack of Christmas presents in front of Les. He was so nice he would probably think it was a hint for charity, and that was the last thing she wanted. She wanted Les to be real with them. That couldn't happen if he saw them as people needing charity. In her experience, no one ever gave charity without looking down on the person they gave it to.

"Santa still needs to do his shopping," Marla said. She vowed she was going to go home and put in an order from the J. C. Penney catalog. She knew by heart the page number that had the Suzy bake set advertised. She'd already decided to get it. And while she was ordering she'd get Sammy a football at the same time.

Maybe if Sammy had a football, Les could throw him a few passes now and then when he came into Dry Creek. That was assuming Les would want to be around any of them once that shepherd was fixed.

Marla looked over at the man. He certainly looked as if he wanted to be around them now.

Les turned on the light in the workshop when he led everyone inside. He was glad he'd spent so much time finishing up this workshop, because he was pleased to be able to share it with Marla and the kids.

"Up there's the tool cabinet and over there's the refrigerator."

"Cool," Sammy said as he looked at the refrigerator. "Do you keep stuff to drink in there?"

Les smiled. "There are usually a few sodas and maybe some canned fruit. But the reason it's there is to hold any medicine I need for the animals."

Sammy was still looking around. "And it's got its own heat. A guy could go camping in here."

"There's even a fold-up cot and a sleeping bag in that closet. Sometimes I sleep out here during calving season."

Les had to admit it felt good to have Sammy share his enthusiasm for the workshop. He supposed that's what a father must feel like a hundred times a day when his son enjoyed something the man had built.

Marla and Becky stayed in the workshop while Sammy went with Les to bring in the damaged shepherd figure.

"You're doing a good job," Les said as Sammy shouldered his full share of the weight of the shepherd. The Nativity figure was plastic, but it was also heavy. Les had parked his pickup next to the barn door and he and Sammy were carrying the shepherd over to the workshop.

"It's slippery," Sammy said.

"We'll need to let it warm up before we start working on it. It's probably brittle from the cold. It's the melting frost that makes it feel damp."

"You sure know a lot about snow."

Les shrugged as best he could given the fact that he was carrying the shepherd's head. "You'll learn all about it, too, after a while. Everyone in Dry Creek becomes an expert on snow."

"I like the sun," Sammy said. "There's nothing to do in the snow."

Les nudged the door to the workshop open with his foot. "Nothing to do? Have you ever heard of a sled?"

Les heard a pickup drive into his place. "That'll be Mr. Morales."

They set the shepherd down on the long table that ran along one side of the workshop.

"I'll go get Mr. Morales. The rest of you stay in here where it's warm."

Les walked outside to greet his friend. The ravine where Mr. Morales had his cabin shared a fence with Les's largest pasture. Mr. Morales usually went to Miles City instead of Dry Creek, but Les meant to invite him to the Christmas Eve sing that the church was doing this year.

The conversation about the Christmas Eve service was still going on when Les and Mr. Morales reached the workshop.

"I need to get to the Dry Creek church more often," Mr. Morales said as he followed Les inside.

"I can't imagine my life without the church," Les agreed as he turned to introduce Mr. Morales to Marla and her kids.

Marla listened to the introductions and made the appropriate responses. But she was thinking about Les's words about the church. She'd never thought the church had anything to offer someone like her, but after listening to what the pastor had said yesterday about Mary, she wasn't so sure. She hadn't realized God cared about humble people. For some reason, she always thought he wanted the rich, popular people to fill his churches. There had never seemed to be any room for her there.

Marla waited until Mr. Morales took the children out to see the lambs before saying something to Les.

"Remember that man Byron in church yesterday?"

Les looked up from the toolbox he was lifting and grunted an acknowledgment.

"I was wondering if he meant it when he said he was available for questions about the church?"

"He's an usher. He passes those cards out to everyone. He's not supposed to be the one answering the questions. He only collects the cards."

"Oh."

"Anyone could answer your questions," Les said, then cleared his throat. "I could probably answer some."

"Oh, I wouldn't want to bother you. You're working on the shepherd today."

"I've got time. Besides, I'm a deacon in the church. Byron is only an usher." Les frowned. "Of course, he's a good usher. If you want to find a place to sit, he's your man."

Marla nodded. She didn't even know what a deacon was, and she didn't want to show her ignorance by asking. She did know what an usher was, though. Maybe she should start off small and talk to him first. "Well, we don't need to do anything today."

"We could make an appointment," Les offered.

Marla nodded. "That would be nice."

"Mrs. Hargrove might be willing to watch the kids so we can talk."

"Oh, I don't know—"

"We could have dinner together. At the café."

There, Les told himself. He had done it. He had asked Marla out on a date. The whole town of Dry Creek would be talking when he showed up in the café to have dinner with her.

"I would pay, of course," Les added when Marla didn't say anything.

Les hated to admit it, but his respect for Byron was growing. It wasn't easy to charm a woman and Les had a sinking feeling that he was failing at it.

"You could have anything on the menu." Les wondered if he should have offered to take her to Miles City. The Dry Creek café had good food, but it never pretended to be an elegant place. Come to think of it, he would have to drive her to Billings to find an elegant place.

"That's very nice," Marla said. "But I would insist on paying for my share. I mean, I'm the one with the questions."

"Oh." Now that Les had gone to the hard work of asking Marla out, he found he definitely wanted it to be a date and not just two people eating dinner together. "I could ask you some questions, too."

The words were out of Les's mouth before he even thought of them. He was sure they were something Byron would say.

"About what?" Marla was frowning now.

"Ah—well, maybe the kids." Les figured that was a safe topic. Women always liked to talk about their children. He'd heard Byron ask mothers at church about their children and it always seemed to go well.

"They're good kids."

Marla was looking at him the way she had the other morning when she was peeking out the crack in the door and he was asking about Becky.

"I know," Les said softly. Then he did what he'd wanted to do that morning when he'd first seen her almost closing the door in his face. He reached out a hand and touched her cheek. "They're great kids."

Marla blushed.

"How about tomorrow night for dinner?"

Marla nodded.

Les decided that the one thing he needed to add to his workshop was a stereo system. He'd like a little music about now.

When Mr. Morales brought the children back they joined in working on the shepherd. They used putty Marla had mixed up to fill in some of the breaks in the shepherd's back. Les was making a brace for the putty so that it would stay in the places they wanted it to and dry right. Sammy helped Mr. Morales mix the right color of paint to match the shepherd's robes.

Marla decided that she hadn't had such a happy time since her husband had died. She had her children with her. They were having a good time. Mr. Morales reminded her of her uncles, and he'd already promised to come visit them when he came into Dry Creek. And then there was Les.

It was four o'clock before they finished for

the day. The putty needed to dry overnight and they planned to paint it tomorrow.

"The shepherd's going to look just fine," Les said as he wiped a little extra putty off the worktable.

Les had eventually covered the worktable with a canvas tarp so that the putty didn't get over everything.

"Would you mind folding the tarp?" Les asked Sammy. "That way I can load some feed up for Mr. Morales to take with him."

Marla held her breath. She knew Les was trusting Sammy with the Nativity figure by leaving him alone with it. She forced herself to add to the trust.

"I'll take Becky inside and get her washed up," Marla said.

Sammy nodded.

Marla noticed her son stood a little taller. Or at least, it looked to her as if he did. A boy needed to be trusted if he was going to turn into a solid young man. She was grateful Les seemed to realize that. Maybe Les really did want to have dinner with her so he could talk about the children. Somehow that thought wasn't as welcome as it had been earlier. Children weren't exactly good date conversation. Oh, well, she'd have several hours tomorrow to talk to him about the children while they all finished up the shepherd. Maybe he'd get his questions answered then and they would have time to talk about other things at dinner.

Chapter Nine

Les sat down at his breakfast table the next morning with several articles spread out in front of him. He'd done a search on his computer and pulled the articles from the digital archives of the *Los Angeles Times*. Any other time, if he had found the information he wanted so quickly, he would be telling himself that he could do anything with his computer beside him. Now, though, he didn't feel like congratulating himself.

Yesterday evening, after he'd finished his chores, Les had gone back into the workshop to be sure that the putty was drying in the cracks of the shepherd's back. He kept a high-wattage bulb in the overhead light in the workshop, so he had no trouble seeing the marks in the corner of his worktable. Someone had taken one of the small paintbrushes and painted "XIX" on the wooden table.

Les had forgotten about the numbers that had been on the note. He'd found out who took the shepherd so fast, he hadn't bothered with any follow-up. It hadn't taken him long with his computer to find out that those numbers were the symbol for the 19th Street gang. The articles in front of him told the rest of the story. Murders, robberies, lots of drugs. The 19th Street gang wasn't a social club.

He wondered how long Sammy had been a member. It said in one of the articles that the gang recruited boys as young as nine. Sammy could be hard core by now.

Les rubbed a hand over his face. No one was who they seemed anymore. He had thought Sammy was some young mischief maker who just needed a little attention. That might be like saying the latest serial killer was just a choirboy who needed a little more applause. If Les had learned anything in his reserve deputy training it was that a lawman couldn't go by stereotypes. He'd made a rookie's mistake. But who would look at an eleven-year-old boy and ask if he was a member of one of the most vicious big-city gangs around?

And who would look at the boy's mother and

ask if she was capable of withholding that kind of information from the local reserve deputy sheriff? Marla had clearly known what that gang symbol meant and she'd kept silent.

Les got up to get another cup of coffee. It was going to be a long day. He might even call in an emergency request to the church's prayer chain. Mrs. Hargrove headed up the prayer chain and he could give her some generalities without saying what was going on. She was good about that. And he could definitely use the help of other believers on this one.

He'd be sure to move that hunting knife he kept in the workshop to another place. Marla and the kids would be back here in a couple of hours. Les wondered if Marla planned to ever tell him about her son. She certainly hadn't made any effort to tell him yesterday while they sat together filling the cracks on the shepherd's back. They had worked away for a good hour while Mr. Morales showed the kids how to feed the lambs. She'd told him this and that about her life in Los Angeles and he'd told her more than he usually told anyone about his childhood. None of what she'd said hinted at something like this, though.

It was too bad, Les told himself as he sat at the table. Trust—and truth—were such vital parts of any relationship. Suddenly, restoring that shepherd didn't seem so important. He supposed he should go out and paint over the gang symbol before everyone got here. That would at least send a signal to Sammy that Les had noticed something.

Not that it would probably mean anything to the boy. He probably didn't know Les had a computer and could find out what the symbol meant. Kids that age never realized what other people knew. It was probably just a gesture of arrogance that made him paint that "XIX" again. Either that or the kid was planning something.

Well, Les told himself, he would be on his guard today. The romantic nonsense had certainly been wiped out of his eyes. He'd be watching the boy. And the mother, too. Little Becky was probably the only one of the family who had been honest with him. Her only goal was to get that Suzy bake set in the deluxe edition.

For the first time that morning Lester smiled. It was a bitter smile, but he felt it inside. He knew how it felt to want something so badly everything else faded away. He and Becky had that in common, at least. Maybe he should just go ahead and order that Suzy bake set online. If he did the rush delivery, it would be here before Christmas. Then at least one of them would get what they wanted. His growing dream of having a family would have to wait.

Marla had brought tortillas and cheese so she could make everyone quesadillas for lunch. She even had a jar of a special salsa she'd brought with her from Los Angeles. She knew Les liked quesadillas and yesterday Mr. Morales had said he liked them, too. She had no idea why no one was eating them now with any enjoyment.

Yesterday had been magical, and today was—well, not.

It was because of Les. She had forgotten how a man who was in a bad mood could influence everyone around him. Not that Les was in a bad mood exactly. He was certainly polite to everyone. And he wasn't snapping at people for doing this or that. It had taken her a minute to figure it all out this morning. Les was never very talkative. He was a quiet man. But he had been a quiet man who seemed to relax into other people. She'd felt more herself around him yesterday than she had felt anywhere in a long time.

Today there was no relaxing. All his walls

were up. He was more official than he had
been when he was knocking at her door inves-
tigating the theft of the shepherd. He'd at least
smiled at her then.

Marla looked at him more closely. He was
sitting at the table opposite Sammy. No one
had said anything for the past minute. Even
Becky was quiet.

"More quesadillas?" Marla finally asked.

"Yes, *gracias*," Mr. Morales said as he held
his plate out. "They are good."

Marla used a fork to serve the older man
another quesadilla. "I'm glad you like them."

At least Mr. Morales was still friendly to
her. She liked being around him. His speech
and mannerisms reminded her so much of
her uncles, and she hadn't seen them in years.
She wrote to them, of course, but her Spanish
wasn't very good. Besides, it wasn't the same
as seeing their faces. She had listened as Mr.
Morales told her children about the life of a
shepherd while they'd worked on the Nativity
figure together this morning.

After everyone had finished eating, there
was no reason to linger in the house.

It was late afternoon before they finished
with the shepherd. The cracks in the figure

had all been filled with putty and painted to match the color of either the shepherd's skin or his garments. Mr. Morales had fashioned a covering from thick paper to repair the hole in the side of the shepherd's head. Several coats of varnish had weatherproofed the paper so it would be able to tolerate the snow.

"You won't be able to tell he was ever broken," Les said as they started to clean up their putty knives and brushes.

"Good," Sammy muttered.

"He'll be dried tomorrow if you want to help me set him back up," Les said to the boy. He felt an urge to help Sammy unscrew the lid on the old jar that held the used paintbrushes. The lid was encrusted with dry paint and didn't open smoothly. But Les wasn't sure the boy would welcome his help.

"I guess," Sammy said.

Les knew the boy was probably disappointed because no one felt the same camaraderie they'd felt yesterday. But yesterday they were all different people.

"Well, we'll put the shepherd back to work," Marla said a little too cheerfully.

"He has to take care of the lambs," Becky added wistfully. "They don't have anyone to take care of them."

Les swallowed. "I've been keeping an eye on them."

"You'll come by our house?" Sammy looked up from the jar.

Les nodded. He supposed he would have to go by and pick the boy up if they were going to set up the shepherd together. "And I'll see you tonight, when I come to pick up your mother for dinner."

"Oh," Marla said. "I thought we'd just meet at the café."

"No, I can come by and pick you up."

Les wondered if the woman didn't want him in her house. It hadn't looked as if she'd had much in the house when he glanced in the other day. But drugs didn't take much room to hide. It might even be normal for drug houses not to have much furniture. Now that he was thinking about it, Marla had shown a definite interest in how much drug use there was in Dry Creek.

Les felt his gut tighten. He hadn't considered until now that she might be a member of that 19th Street gang herself. She could have gotten involved in the gang with that dead husband of hers. One of the articles he'd read said that happened more often than people knew. Come to think of it, she'd never said how her husband had died. She'd never said how she made a living, either.

He thought back to when he'd sat with her on that old log behind her house. He'd told her everything she needed to know about crime in Dry Creek. She had played him for a fool. He should have just given her the keys to the city and been done with it.

He wondered if she had agreed to have dinner with him so she could find out more about criminal prospects in Dry Creek. It would be useful if she meant to set up a drug business behind the law's back. He knew most people in Dry Creek would say no to drugs, but there were bound to be some kids who would say yes. It was his job to protect those kids.

Les wondered how it was possible to dread a dinner so much and still have the thought of it bring out every longing he had. The only good thing was that he didn't have any more town secrets left to tell her and she probably wasn't interested in his personal secrets.

"I'll see you at six, then," Marla finally said. She didn't look any happier about dinner than he did, Les thought. But it didn't matter; they were going to go on a date.

There was a little more silence as they all just looked at the shepherd figure.

"He doesn't look very strong," Sammy finally said.

"Oh, he's strong," Mr. Morales said. "All shepherds are strong. They have to be. They protect the lambs from wolves and other things."

"Oh," Becky said, and then gave an anxious look to Les.

"Don't worry," he said. "There aren't any wolves around Dry Creek. They don't like to come into towns. You're safe. The lambs by the church are safe."

"Even if wolves got to Dry Creek, you would shoot them with your rifle, wouldn't you?" Sammy asked.

Les looked into the boy's eyes at that comment. Either the boy was a very good actor or he was scared of something. Somehow, Les doubted it was the wolves. "Usually we try to trap wolves instead of shooting them, but— yes—if there is no other way, and someone is in danger, we will shoot them."

Sammy relaxed. "Those sheep by the church are plastic, anyway."

Les nodded. "They certainly have no worries."

"You'll have to bring your pickup with you tonight, won't you?" Sammy asked.

Les nodded. "I guess."

He usually used his pickup when he went into Dry Creek in the winter. In the summer months he didn't have to worry about traction on the road, so he used his car more often. Roads, even his gravel road, tended to get slippery in the winter after the sun went down.

Les looked at Sammy again. The boy was rubbing his hands along the hem of the shepherd's cloak. There had been no damage there and there were no cracks to be filled.

"Is there something wrong?" Les finally asked.

Sammy looked up and shook his head.

Well, Les told himself, he had tried to reach the boy. If he was a seasoned gang member, a little bit of concern wouldn't stop him from his plans, anyway.

For the first time all week Les wished the regular sheriff were back. Les had been prepared to arrest someone when the sheriff was gone; he hadn't been prepared to have it mean anything to him, though. He hadn't realized until now that the regular sheriff had such a tough job. No wonder the sheriff had wanted to go to Maui.

Chapter Ten

Marla looked inside her closet and hoped something new would be there. Unfortunately, all she saw were the same T-shirts and blouses she always saw when she opened her closet. For the first time ever, she wished she'd had jobs in her life that required a woman to wear a dress. Maybe then she would have something suitable to wear to dinner with the deputy sheriff.

It suddenly hit her. She was going for a date for the first time in almost sixteen years. Not that it was a real date. There wouldn't be any hand-holding or kissing. Would there be? Oh, dear, she hadn't kissed a man except for her husband in the past sixteen years, either.

Marla looked around. She needed to relax. If the sheriff was anything like the way he had been this afternoon, there wouldn't even be any friendly conversation to worry about.

The only thing in her closet to wear that wasn't jeans was that black suit. Oh, and her fiesta blouse and skirt, but she wasn't going to wear that, especially not on a cold winter night. She'd look totally out of place. And it would look as if she expected a party, which she didn't. It was only dinner.

Finally Marla decided to wear her newest pair of jeans and a chocolate-brown sweater. It looked casual and—well, casual was probably the best thing she could say about it. She stood in front of the mirror in the bathroom and added a thin gold necklace that her husband had given her one year for Christmas.

She lifted her hair and twisted it back, but then decided to leave it hanging straight. She had never been a woman who dressed elegantly and there was no hope of starting now. It was just that having a touch of glamour about her might make her feel more confident.

Her eyes were clear, though, and she had on a light lipstick. She put a dab of perfume behind one ear and a tissue in her pocket. She was ready. And she had twenty minutes to wait before Les would be there.

Marla left the bathroom and walked into

the dining room. Sammy and Becky were sitting together at the folding table playing a card game called Birds.

Marla felt her nervousness leave her. Now, this was what was important in her life. She needed reminders like this that Sammy cared about his sister. He was a good boy. Moving to Dry Creek had been the best decision she had made in a long time. "You can take the game with you when you go over to Mrs. Hargrove's, if you want. It'll keep you busy."

"I don't know why we have to go to a babysitter's," Sammy muttered as he looked up at her.

"Becky's only four. She needs someone to watch her," Marla said as she walked over to where they sat. "You're going along so Becky doesn't feel alone. And to help Mrs. Hargrove with Becky."

Sammy rolled his eyes. "I don't think that lady needs any help. You should see her with those Sunday-school kids. They don't even want to get into trouble."

Marla put her hand on Sammy's shoulder. "I'm proud of you for helping in that Sunday-school class."

Sammy didn't shrug off her hand. Instead, he looked up at her. "Is this something you're going to be doing a lot? This going out with the deputy sheriff?"

"Oh, I wouldn't say we're going out," Marla protested. "We're just getting together to have dinner. And it's only this one time."

Marla remembered now that this had all started because she had some questions she wanted to ask about the Dry Creek church. She should have put a stop to this dinner before it went this far. She could have just gone over to Mrs. Hargrove's house with the kids and asked the older woman her questions. She'd rather talk to Mrs. Hargrove than Les any day. That is, if Les was going to be all stiff around her as he had been today. She had liked talking to him on Monday; he'd been friendly then.

"The sheriff's not so bad," Sammy said as he looked back down at the Bird cards he held in his hands. "At least, he knows how to do lots of stuff."

"Is he going to be our new daddy?" Becky looked up as she asked.

Marla flushed. She supposed her children weren't any more comfortable with her going on a date than she was. "We're just going to dinner. It's barely a date. People don't get married after just one date."

"How many dates did you have with Dad?" Sammy asked. "Before you got married?"

"I don't remember."

"More than ten?"

Marla nodded. "Many more than ten. So you don't need to worry about the sheriff."

"I wasn't worried."

"Well, good, because you don't need to be."

There was a minute of silence.

"He walks you home, though, doesn't he?" Sammy asked suddenly. He glanced up at Marla and then back at his cards.

"Oh, I don't know. I don't think it particularly matters."

"You don't want to come home alone when the house is all dark," Sammy said emphatically. "It could be creepy then. You need to ask him to walk you home."

"Well, if we do anything, we'll probably just walk over to Mrs. Hargrove's and then walk back from there," Marla said. "It's not far."

"Then he could walk us all home," Sammy said with satisfaction. "We should leave some lights on in the house, too. So when we get home, it's not dark."

Marla looked at her son. She still had her hand resting on his shoulder and she gave him a squeeze. Something was going on. Maybe it was the move itself that was making him feel so vulnerable. He'd never given this much thought to darkness in his whole life. "Are you worried about something?"

Sammy shook his head.

Marla looked at him some more. "They don't have many streetlights in Dry Creek, do they? Not like they have in Los Angeles."

Marla had never seen darkness as deep as the nights she'd spent in Montana. She liked it because she could see the stars, but she could understand how a child might not find the night comforting.

"I'm not afraid of the dark," Sammy muttered as he stared at his cards.

"Well, we'll talk about it later if you want."

"Isn't it time for us to go over to Mrs. Hargrove's?" Sammy asked as he folded his hand of cards.

Marla supposed that, whatever Sammy's problems were, they could wait until the morning. The best time to talk to Sammy was at breakfast. Maybe she'd make them pancakes tomorrow and spend some extra time just sitting with him. Sammy was never one to confide his problems easily. In the meantime, he was right. It was time to get everyone ready to go over to Mrs. Hargrove's house.

* * *

Les had known his dinner date would cause a little gossip in Dry Creek. Any date seemed to be prime news, and he hadn't asked a woman out in over a year. He'd expected Mrs. Hargrove to tell Linda, and maybe Charley, that she was babysitting the children so he and Marla could have dinner together.

But even knowing all that, Les was surprised at how much work Linda had done. Usually, if Linda suspected a couple was on a date, she put a candle on their table. When he and Marla stepped into the café, however, they stepped into a Christmas fantasyland. There were twinkling Christmas lights everywhere. Since Elmer had worried about the electricity the church was using, Les hoped the older man didn't see this.

"Oh," Marla said with pleasure in her voice. "I like Christmas lights."

Les liked Christmas lights, too. He just wasn't sure he wanted a thousand of them shining down on him while he ate his steak.

Linda had draped strands of blinking white lights from the pipe that hung down in the middle of the room and they spread out to hit every corner. They were hooked to every side of the room, too. And a dozen places in between.

"It's beautiful," Marla said.

Les nodded. The lights throbbed. He wondered how much wattage was in the room. Fortunately, the lights were all white, so at least the glare was even.

Les took another step into the café so the door could swing closed behind them. "It's warm."

It was cold outside and Les felt the air inside the café take away the slight chill that had come from walking the children over to Mrs. Hargrove's place and then walking Marla back to the café. He had parked his pickup at Marla's. It seemed pointless to drive when everything was so close.

"Does she do this every Christmas?" Marla whispered as she slowly twirled around to see all the lights.

"No, she doesn't."

Marla had a look of such childish wonder on her face that in an instant Les forgave everyone for meddling in his date. It was almost impossible to look at Marla's face and reconcile her with the picture of a drug-dealing female gang member that had been bothering him all day.

"Linda did it for us," Les said softly as he motioned Marla forward.

There was only one choice for a table. Sitting in the middle of the café, there was a table draped in a white tablecloth, with a vase holding a long-stemmed red rose in the center. The table was sitting under the pipe that came down from the ceiling, so all the lights gathered to that one point. It was like sitting in the middle of a huge circus tent.

"I've never had anyone do something like this for me," Marla said as she stepped toward the table.

Les swallowed. Marla was the kind of woman men should have slain dragons for. What kind of man had her husband been that she had never felt special like this before? Even if he was into drugs and crime, couldn't the man have put some effort into letting his wife know that she was beautiful?

"You look nice tonight," Les said as he held out a chair for Marla.

Les had barely sat down himself when he heard the music start. At first he assumed it was a CD playing on the stereo system Linda had in the kitchen. On other special occasions in the past, she had turned up the volume and cranked out everything from romantic waltz music to Christmas carols. There was a roughness to the quality of the music, though, that made him wonder.

When Les turned around, he was shocked. There was Elmer, wearing a suit and playing a harp. Les recognized the suit; Elmer wore it to funerals. He didn't usually wear a tie, though, and tonight the older man was cinched tight with a black tie.

The harp looked like the secondhand instrument Mrs. Hargrove had asked the church to buy for a past Christmas program. No one had played the thing in the program. Elmer was making a valiant attempt to play it now. He gave Les a smile and a brief thumbs-up sign between strums.

When Linda came out wearing her chef's hat, Les wasn't even surprised. Nothing was normal tonight.

"I didn't know we still had that harp," Les said when Linda handed him a menu.

"Oh, yes," Linda said as she handed another menu to Marla.

Les thought Linda might elaborate, but she didn't. The café owner just stood there with a proud smile on her face as though she had single-handedly wrought a miracle.

"New menu?" Les guessed.

"I thought you might like the Asian pork loin."

Les nodded. No one got away with ordering

a hamburger when they were having a date at Linda's café. "Sounds good to me."

"I have a gallon of spiced apple cider chilling in the back, too. Just in case you'd like to make a toast."

Les looked at Marla. She was pink with pleasure. "How about it? Do you want to try the cider? Linda gets it in specially from Washington."

"Yes, please. It all sounds wonderful."

Linda smiled. "I want this to be a night you both remember."

Les figured he, for one, wasn't likely to forget it.

"I just wanted some information about the church," Marla said.

Linda smiled even wider. "Mrs. Hargrove will know all that. She does the flower arrangements when we have them in front of the altar."

Les was starting to think things weren't adding up right.

"I'm surprised you don't do the flowers," Marla said. "You've decorated your café beautifully. It looks like we're sitting here under a chandelier."

"Or a diamond," Linda agreed as she started to turn to walk back to the kitchen. Before she made her full turn, though, she stopped for a second and winked at Les.

It suddenly all came together in Les's mind. He'd given Mrs. Hargrove that cryptic prayer request this morning. He hadn't said much except he had an important decision to make today and it could have life-altering consequences, so he wanted to be sure he was on solid ground before he took any steps.

He wanted the people of Dry Creek to pray about whether or not he should get a search warrant for Marla's house to see if she was hiding any drugs. Instead, they had put it together with his date tonight and thought he was going to propose here and now. The toast. The harp. Elmer's suit. It all added up. No wonder Elmer was sitting over there grinning at him.

"The church is made up of God's people," Les said to Marla as he moved the candle so he could lean closer. "Sometimes that's a good thing. Sometimes it's a real pain. But if you want to know about the church, all you have to do is ask."

Then he reached over and took her hand in his.

All the butterflies in Marla's stomach relaxed when Les took her hand. She was worried that the people here tonight were trying to make more of the dinner she and Les were having than Les was comfortable with. But when he took her hand, she knew he was okay with it all. However it had happened, they were on a date that wasn't just a dinner. And the man in question was fine with it.

"I don't know much about church," Marla began, then took a deep breath. "But my husband had this cross. When he was sick, he used to look at it."

Marla told Les everything. She hadn't planned to tell him it all. She thought she'd just ask about why her husband had been able to wring meaning from that wooden cross and she hadn't been able to get so much as a warm feeling from it.

Instead, one question led to another, and she told him about her husband's confession to her before he died. She told him about the anger she felt because she'd had no time to even ask her husband any questions about his confession. She didn't know why he'd been unfaithful. She stopped short of asking him if he thought there was something wrong with her as a woman. Maybe her anguish showed in her eyes, though.

"Your husband was a fool," Les said. They'd both received their plates some time ago and the food was growing cold. Les didn't seem to care. "He didn't deserve a woman like you."

Marla blinked back a tear. "Thank you."

Les felt a tear in his own eye. He knew God was merciful. Somehow, no matter what this woman in front of him had done, she had a sweetness that a man could put his faith in. She still hadn't told him anything about why her family was involved with this gang, but he was sure there was a good reason.

The café had remained empty except for the two of them. Les knew Linda was turning away customers, because several times the door had opened and she had stepped over to have muted conversations with whoever it was. Finally Elmer had given up on playing the harp and moved out to the porch to stall any hungry people.

Les should have cared about how much inconvenience he was causing his neighbors. But he knew Linda was giving people take-out containers from the back door, so at least no one was starving. And for tonight, he liked having the privacy. Marla had shown him her grief. He'd answered with emotions he hadn't even known he had.

He knew he should ask her about the gang symbols her son was leaving everywhere. He probably should even ask her if she did drugs herself. But tonight he didn't want to be Les Wilkerson, Reserve Deputy Sheriff. He didn't even want to be Les Wilkerson, upright citizen. He just wanted to be a man telling a woman she was beautiful in his eyes.

"You should eat," Marla finally said to him. "Your dinner's getting cold."

Les smiled. "Linda buys to-go containers by the boxful. But you should eat."

Neither one of them seemed ready to take up a fork, so Les reached over and took Marla's hand again.

Linda had either unplugged some of the Christmas lights or half the strands had burned out. Whatever the reason, he and Marla no longer sat under a spotlight. In fact, the twinkling lights overhead were quite romantic.

"You know I wrote a poem," Les said. "About your hair."

Marla reached up with her free hand and touched her hair. "I don't have enough highlights."

"Your hair is beautiful."

Marla smiled.

Les breathed deeply. All was well with the world.

Then he heard some loud muttering out on

the porch. It had been going on for the past minute or two, but Les had figured it was just one of the ranch hands who wanted to come inside to eat and didn't want to go around back for a takeout.

It couldn't be that, though. He frowned, then turned to face the door. He recognized Mrs. Hargrove's voice.

"It's Sammy," Mrs. Hargrove said as she finally opened the door. The older woman and Becky walked into the café and Mrs. Hargrove didn't even turn around to close the door. A cold wind blew inside. In the time Les and Marla had been sitting there, the sky had turned to deep night. It must be almost eight o'clock.

Marla stood up. "What?"

"I can't find him," Mrs. Hargrove said. The scarf was off her head and she looked distraught. "I've looked everywhere."

"Well, he has to be around here," Marla said. She stepped away from the table and walked toward the café door. "Did you look at our house?"

Les stood and followed Marla.

Mrs. Hargrove nodded. "It's all dark there."

"But we left the lights on," Marla protested. "Surely he's not sitting by himself in the dark."

Les walked over to the coatrack and got Marla's coat. He picked up his own while he was there.

"Wherever he's gone to, we'll find him," Les said as he held Marla's coat for her to put on. There were not many places to hide in Dry Creek, not even for an eleven-year-old boy.

Linda came out of the kitchen wiping her hands on a towel. "Maybe he's visiting with those friends of his. The two guys that stopped to give him back his baseball."

"His baseball!" Marla said, and Les saw her face go white.

In that word, Marla had gone from worried to terrified. Les wished for the first time tonight that he hadn't let Marla's eyes distract him from what he needed to do. He had to ask her about her past.

"Are they from the 19th Street gang?"

Marla stared at him. "You know?"

Any hope Les had that Marla had no connection with the gang died. He nodded. "I know."

"We have to find Sammy," Marla said as she turned to the door. "I don't know if that's where they're from or not."

Elmer came inside and looked at Les. "What's wrong?"

"Mrs. Hargrove. You and Becky stay here." Les turned to Elmer. "Get everyone inside and lock the doors. And turn out those Christmas tree lights. People are in a fishbowl in here if someone looks in the windows."

Elmer nodded.

"And pray," Les asked. He looked at Mrs. Hargrove, Elmer, Linda and Becky all huddled together by now in the middle of the room. "Pray and pray."

"I'll go with you," Marla said as Les walked to the door.

Les hesitated. "Do you know these guys?"

"They're with my son," Marla said. "I have to go."

Les nodded. He didn't know if it was better to have her with him or not. The only thing he knew for sure was that he could watch her better if he had her with him. He had no idea what the guys really brought to Dry Creek. If the "baseball" was code for a drug shipment, he might have to confront Marla before the night was out. It was highly unlikely two guys would be bringing a drug shipment to an eleven-year-old boy unless the boy's parent was also part of the deal.

Chapter Eleven

It took them an hour to work their way through Dry Creek. Les knocked at the door of each house and asked if anyone had seen any strangers. At each place, the people inside said no. Les cautioned everyone to lock their doors and stay inside tonight. Then he searched the church and the hardware store.

"He's got to be here. Someone's lying," Marla finally said.

They had come back to the middle of the street in front of the café. The ground was frozen, but there was no new snow, so it was impossible to tell if any unknown vehicles had come through town.

There had been no other conversation between them since they had started looking. Once, when he saw that Marla's fingers were getting cold, Les had taken off his gloves and given them to her, but neither one of them had spoken.

"My neighbors don't lie," Les said. *Unlike some people I know*, he almost added, but didn't. He knew the less said the better. He needed to keep his mind focused and forget about his heart. If she was part of some drug-delivery scheme, he might need to arrest her before the night was over. He didn't think he could do it if he allowed his feelings to show.

The one streetlight in Dry Creek shone above them. Les could see how the cold had made Marla's cheeks turn rosy. Her lips were chapped and it looked as if she might have been crying at some point tonight.

"Would Sammy run away with these guys?" Les asked.

"No!"

Les looked at Marla. The one thing he knew for sure about her was that she cared for her children.

"I'll get my pickup and drive down the road a bit."

"I'm coming with you."

Les nodded. It did seem that, whether they wanted to be or not, they were tied together for tonight. Les heard his boots crunch on the frozen ground. Marla's footsteps were more muffled, though. He looked down and saw that she was wearing some kind of thin dress shoes. Her feet must feel like blocks of ice.

"We've got time to stop at your place so you can change shoes."

"I'm fine," Marla said. "You don't need to stop for me."

Les didn't argue. He just walked past his pickup, which was parked in her driveway, and kept going until he reached Marla's front door. "I can wait here while you get your shoes."

It wasn't politeness that made Les wait. He knew if he went inside Marla's house again he would be looking for places where she could hide illegal substances. Of course, he would be limited in that. He'd rather just wait until he had a search warrant.

Marla nodded and took a key out of her pocket to open the door. The lights were on in every room. They had already looked into the rooms of the house earlier and had left the lights on. It was the first place they had gone after they left the café.

Les watched Marla enter the living room and then he realized the guys could have circled back. "Wait. I'm coming."

Les cleared each room before he let Marla enter it. He'd have to protect her if he arrested her, anyway. He might as well start now. He watched as Marla reached into her closet and pulled out a pair of tennis shoes.

He frowned. "Do you have some heavy socks to go with those?"

Marla shook her head. "But my regular socks do fine."

Les shook his head. He never understood why people would move to Montana and not buy some thick socks. Those socks she was holding were meant for the summer.

"Here. Sit on the bed," Les said. He didn't want to have someone trailing along behind him with a case of frostbite developing. He'd probably have to see to that, too, if he arrested her.

Les took off Marla's shoes and pulled off the thin socks she was wearing. Then he put his hands around her right foot. He kept his hands there until her skin had warmed and then he began to rub her feet gently, just enough to get the circulation going.

He tried not to wonder why Marla was holding herself so stiff.

Marla knew why women sometimes ran off with an unlikely man. He rubbed their feet. Ahhhh, that felt good even with the shooting tingle. She held herself steady, though. She didn't want Les to know how she was feeling. His hands were warm and he cradled the one foot while he started rubbing the other one. It wasn't right that a man who didn't trust a woman could rub her feet.

"We should be going," Marla said.

"We're almost done."

In another minute, Les put her socks on and then he put her tennis shoes on and tied them. He even held her steady for the first couple of minutes while she stood in place. After that, it was quick work walking back through the house.

"You should turn your furnace on before we go," Les said as they walked through the living room. "It'll be cold as ice in here by the time you get back."

Marla flushed. She didn't want to admit that they had no gas in the tank for the furnace. She'd been using the fireplace. "We'll be fine. You don't need to worry about us."

Les grunted as he opened the door, but he didn't say anything else.

Marla wasn't sure that Les was as worried about Sammy as she was. The way Les had questioned everyone in the houses around, it was clear he was looking for those two strangers more than he was looking for Sammy. How did he know that Sammy was even with those guys? Maybe he'd seen them and gone into hiding?

Marla stepped onto the porch and turned to lock her door. She supposed locking it now was only habit. The only things of value in her house were her two children, and neither one was home.

Something was not right about Sammy's departure, though. Just because two guys from his old gang had shown up, it didn't mean that Sammy would choose to go off with them. She thought he'd learned a lot since they had come to Dry Creek. He'd even gone to Sunday school.

Marla followed Les to his pickup.

Why would a boy Sammy's age go off with a couple of... Marla hesitated. She didn't really know what to call the two young men. Linda had said they were both Hispanic and wore bandannas around their heads. They seemed to be around sixteen or seventeen years old and Linda had thought she saw a couple of big motorcycles on the other side of the street.

Sammy loved motorcycles, she remembered with a sinking heart. And he'd been forced to go to Sunday school, so anything he learned there he probably considered meaningless.

And he missed his *amigos*. Still, he knew better than to go off with two strangers, anyway, didn't he?

Les walked to the passenger side of the pickup and opened the door for Marla.

Marla was not used to anyone opening doors for her. "Thank you."

Les grunted.

Even being in the cab of the pickup was warmer than being outside. Marla was glad they were driving for the next part of the search. She assumed the truck had a heater that worked and that Les was not hesitant to use it.

She wondered if Sammy was cold, wherever he was. She wondered if those two strangers would think to keep him warm. Then she wondered if the two strangers weren't really strangers after all. Maybe Sammy considered them his best *amigos*. Maybe Sammy had even invited them to come here before he left Los Angeles.

Maybe Les was right about her son after all, Marla thought. She looked over when she heard the latch on the other door click.

Les opened the door on the driver side and started to step up into the cab. He was halfway in when he stopped and stared at something behind Marla's head.

"My rifle's gone."

Marla had never been in Les's pickup before, but she'd seen where men around here put their rifles. They had a gun rack on the inside of the rear window. She turned and looked, and he was right. There was no rifle.

"Maybe you forgot it at home."

Les shook his head. "The only time the rifle leaves its place there is when I've pulled it out to clean it or use it."

Marla drew in her breath. She knew what he was thinking. "Sammy wouldn't have taken it."

"He sure has asked about it often enough."

"But that's just natural young boy curiosity. You know how young boys are."

Les turned to look at her. She thought he might even feel sorry for her. "He took the rifle, Marla. That's not some prank like the shepherd, even. That's theft of a firearm. I'll have to call it in to the county sheriff."

"But you are the sheriff."

"I can't just ignore this, if that's what you're thinking."

"No, I know," Marla said softly. "But maybe it's not the way you think. Maybe the other guys took the rifle."

Les snorted. "They wouldn't have even

known it was there. I doubt they happened to just be looking in old pickups."

"They could have been," Marla insisted stubbornly.

Les didn't say anything for a minute.

"You said it wasn't loaded, anyway," Marla added. "I'm surprised they didn't just leave it here."

Les nodded. "They must have thought they knew where they could get the bullets for it."

"It's the middle of the night. Even if they went into Miles City, there wouldn't be a store that would be open."

Les shook his head. "They're not heading for a store. They're heading for my place."

Marla's protest died on her lips. Could Les be right?

"Sammy already knows the way. He's been there twice." Les hesitated. "Besides, he put his mark on my place."

Marla looked up.

"The XIX sign. He painted it on my worktable out in the barn. I saw it last night after you'd left. Maybe he already had my place picked out."

Marla bowed her head. She had no protests left. Les believed her son was guilty.

"He could be hurt," Marla finally said. "He's not very big for his age. I think that's why…"

She didn't bother to finish. What did it matter why Sammy had gotten involved with the 19th Street gang?

"I just hope—" Marla continued, then stopped.

"Mothers are supposed to hope," Les finally said gruffly. "And with God, all things are possible, so I'm not one to deny anyone the right to hope."

Marla nodded. She wondered if Mrs. Hargrove would pray for Sammy tonight as she had when he was on top of that woodpile. Of course, when the older woman prayed the first time, she had not known Sammy was suspected of any wrongdoing. Marla doubted very many church women would pray for a gang member who was loose in the community around them.

"I'll go to the café and call it in for backup," Les said. "Then I'll decide what to do."

"Please don't hurt Sammy."

"I never hurt anyone if I can help it."

Marla sat quiet. She had to know. "You're going to get another gun to take, aren't you?"

Les was silent for a moment. "I need to assume they're armed and dangerous. I will need a gun if I hope to control the situation."

Marla felt colder inside than she had felt all evening, even when she was outside. She thought she'd been worried when it looked as if Sammy was guilty. But it was nothing to the worry she felt now that he might be shot.

This is exactly why she had moved to Dry Creek. This little town was supposed to protect her son. What had she done wrong?

Les drove over to the café. The lights in the window were still off, and he had to knock loudly on the door and identify himself before anyone came to let them in.

Linda opened the door. A stream of light came from the kitchen doorway. Marla noticed that the plates were still on the table from when she and Les had started to have dinner. Only a few bites had been taken from each meal. The Christmas lights were dark and now the black wires connecting them all to the center looked like spider legs. The evening had gone from a fantasy to a nightmare in just over an hour.

"We're all back in the kitchen," Linda said as she shut and locked the door behind them.

"Becky?" Marla asked as she let Les walk ahead of them.

"She's taking a nap on Elmer's coat." Linda smiled at her.

"Thank you." Marla reminded herself that everyone didn't know what was going on. She was sure Linda wouldn't still be smiling at her when she discovered Les thought Sammy had stolen a gun.

Marla heard Les on the telephone when she followed Linda into the kitchen. He was trying to muffle his words some, but the kitchen wasn't that big and everyone could hear what he was saying. Marla was hesitant to look anyone in the eye, but she had to.

She turned to Mrs. Hargrove. "Would it be okay for Becky to spend the night with you? I can't leave her alone in the house and—"

"Of course," Mrs. Hargrove said as she stood up from the small table where she'd been sitting. She put her hand on Marla's arm. "My daughter's old room is always ready for a guest. It will be my pleasure."

"Sammy's in trouble," Marla blurted out as she looked up into the older woman's eyes. "I don't know how to pray, but…"

"We'll pray together," Mrs. Hargrove said as she opened her arms.

Marla went into the hug.

"Our Father who art in heaven," Mrs. Hargrove began to murmur into Marla's ear. Each word calmed Marla's fears more. She didn't even notice when Les finished his phone call and came over to stand beside her.

Marla wondered if Mrs. Hargrove had a wooden cross hanging somewhere. The older woman seemed to expect more of God than anyone Marla had ever known.

"Thank you," Marla said when the prayer was finished and she had stepped away from the hug.

Mrs. Hargrove nodded. "Don't you worry about Becky. I'll take good care of her."

"I know."

There was a moment's silence.

Then Linda spoke. She was looking at the floor and her voice was muted. "I feel so bad. It's all my fault. I should have had sense enough to realize those two guys were bad news. I just didn't want to interrupt and—"

"It's all right." Les put his hand on the young woman's arm. "We've all made mistakes tonight. We can't go around putting the blame on anyone."

Except for me, Marla thought. She knew Les blamed her. It didn't help any that she blamed herself, too. She must have missed some clue that Sammy was corresponding with his old *amigos*. She remembered the letter about the baseball, but Sammy had said it was nothing. He hadn't even answered it. She doubted he had a stamp to mail a letter, and there was no place to buy a stamp in Dry Creek. She hadn't even had any stamps most of the time since they'd been here. The few times she'd had a letter she'd waited until she needed to drive to Miles City and then mailed it at the post office there.

Marla mentally shook herself. She couldn't be worried about a stamp. Not when Les was quietly talking to Elmer in the other room and she thought she heard the word *tonight*.

Chapter Twelve

"They'll back us up," Les said to Elmer. The two men were leaning on the side counter in the café. Neither had bothered to turn the main light on. They were content with the soft rectangle of light spilling out from the kitchen. "There's just no way for them to get in close enough without being seen."

For the first time ever, Les was grateful that his home was built in a dip in the landscape. His backup from the sheriff's department in Miles City should be able to come within a mile of his place before they had to shut off their car lights. It was that last mile or so, though, that was making it difficult to come up with a plan.

"No one can see to drive down that road at night, not if they turn their headlights off. There's too many ruts. And it's too far to walk in the dark," Les continued. There was some moonlight tonight, but the moon wasn't full. If it hadn't been for the streetlight, he and Marla would have had a hard time walking around Dry Creek in the darkness.

Elmer nodded. The older man had ranched in the area all his life and Les respected his opinion on how to get around at any time of year, but particularly in the winter months.

"I'd say it'll snow before long out there," Elmer added. "And even without snow, that slope leading into your place is slippery in the middle of the night. Don't know of many men who could do it without even a flashlight to help them."

Les was almost sure Sammy had taken the two strangers to his place. It was the only place Sammy knew how to find, and he also knew Les wasn't going to be home in the early part of the evening. It made an ideal hiding place.

Les felt he had let the people of Dry Creek down. He should have questioned Sammy earlier today about his relationship with the 19th Street gang. He should have asked him if anyone was coming who would pose a threat to the people of this town. Although Sammy could easily have lied, so maybe it wouldn't have made any difference.

"I don't think they'll stay long at my place. They're probably just interested in finding some bullets for that rifle."

Elmer nodded. "But they'll stay the night. They probably think no one checks their barns at night. The boy doesn't know any other place to take them, anyway. Not in the dark."

"His name's Sammy." Les didn't like the thought of Sammy being reduced to first "the boy" and then just a number in some juvenile center.

"Huh?" Elmer flushed.

"Never mind," Les muttered. It wasn't his choice, or Elmer's, either, that would put Sammy in detention. Sammy had made his own choices; if he lost his name that was his doing.

Besides, he had more people to think about than Sammy. He knew that the black of night would probably stop the trio from exploring too much until the sun rose. But tomorrow would be a different story. All they would have to do would be to find a gravel road and follow it a mile or two to until they reached someone's home.

"Someone's got to stop them tonight," Elmer said as if he wasn't sure Les agreed. "Tomorrow they'll be able to head over to the Redfern place. You know Chrissy Redfern is alone in the house with her new baby these days. I heard Reno is driving that truck route for his sister. Their place isn't far from yours. It wouldn't take them guys long to find it if they just head out from your place tomorrow and make that left turn. I don't see them driving up to the Elkton ranch because of its size. But if they go the other direction, there's Mrs. Nolan alone on that place of hers. Now that her son's gone, she'd be an easy target."

Les held up his hand. He'd already thought of each of his neighbors. "Believe me, I know."

The theft of his rifle had changed everything.

The sheriff in Miles City had agreed with him that something had to be done tonight. They were both responsible for the well-being of the people in this part of the state and there was no limit to the damage two—or maybe three—armed gang members could do if they went around to the smaller ranches. A lot of people still didn't even lock their doors during the day.

"There's no question that we're going," Les said. They had to. "We just need to figure out what the best way is to get a few men into my place tonight without them being seen."

"Horseback," Elmer said without hesitation. "A horse is the only animal that can walk down that slope of yours without needing even a flashlight."

Les nodded. It was certainly worth considering. "We could come in from the Redfern side. That fence between our two places runs fairly close to the draw leading down to my place. I don't know how many horses they have that would make the ride, though."

Elmer shrugged. "We could always call over to the Elkton place. The boys there would be happy to join us."

The Elkton ranch was the only one of the ranches that had a large crew of workers still. The other places might hire summer help, but the men at the Elkton were seasoned year-round ranch hands. They were Montana men to the core. Les knew he could count on them if he found himself in a tight situation.

"I'm going to call them now," Les said as he headed back toward the kitchen.

Marla stepped out of the kitchen before Les reached the doorway.

"You need to take me with you," she said.

There wasn't enough light to see her eyes, but Les felt the despair in them, anyway. He would stake his life on the fact that she was worried about her son. What he didn't know was whether she was worried about him because he was innocent or because he was guilty.

Les shook his head. "It's too dangerous."

"I'll sign a waiver saying you're not responsible if I'm hurt."

Les looked at her. "You think I'm worried about a *lawsuit*?"

Marla lifted her chin. "If you're taking guns with you, I'm going."

Les wondered when his life had become so complicated. Elmer was standing behind him, not even bothering to pretend he wasn't listening. Mrs. Hargrove was eyeing him through the doorway of the kitchen. Les supposed if his friends hadn't given him any privacy when they thought he was proposing marriage, he couldn't expect them to give him any now.

"It's because of the guns that you can't go." Les held up his hand. "And not just the guns we have. It's the gun we know they have, too."

"They don't even have bullets."

"I keep bullets in one of the drawers in the workshop," Les said. "I have them on the top shelf in my closet, too. It won't take them long to find bullets."

Les didn't add that Sammy might already

have found the bullets when he was working in the workshop on that shepherd figure.

Marla might have come to the same realization, because she bit her lip. "All the more reason for me to go."

Les shook his head.

"If you don't take me with you, I'll go, anyway. I know the way to your place. I've already driven there two times."

"I can't let you do that."

Marla stepped back, but her voice was still strong. "You can't stop me. Not unless you're going to arrest me or something. Is that what you're going to do? If you are, you might as well do it now."

Marla put her hands out as if she was ready for handcuffs.

Les didn't even carry handcuffs. "You know I don't have enough to arrest you on."

Les heard an indignant gasp, and this one wasn't from Marla.

"Lester Wilkerson, I can't believe you would seriously consider arresting Marla," Mrs. Hargrove said as she stepped out of the kitchen. "Not when you're planning to propose to her."

"Oh."

"Oh."

There was a chorus of surprised female reactions and one startled grunt from Elmer.

"I'm sorry. I shouldn't have said—" Mrs. Hargrove began.

"But he hasn't asked yet, has he?" Linda interrupted. "No one's drunk the cider."

Les just looked at the two women. "When someone makes an unspoken prayer request, that doesn't mean people can speak out what they think it might mean in some fantasy. Unspoken is unspoken. I wasn't talking about proposing to anyone."

"Oh." That one came from Marla.

She was holding herself too still. Les felt her tension. Whoever she was and whatever her relationship was to that gang, she was so close to tears she could barely keep them in. Les could see her struggle.

"Not that whoever gets your promise to marry him won't be one very fortunate man," Les said softly.

Now that Mrs. Hargrove and Linda had done their damage, they slid back into the kitchen like cowards, dragging Elmer with them.

"I'm still going with you," Marla whispered. Her eyes were black pools of determination. "You can't keep me away."

Les nodded. What she asked for was probably against a hundred regulations and the regular sheriff would have Les's badge when he heard about it, but Les was still going to do it. He had no doubt Marla would head out to his place on her own. If she wasn't in league with those two strangers, she could end up getting shot. If she was working with them, they'd know he was coming and he could be shot.

"You'll stay with me, though," Les said. "And when I say duck, you duck. You'll be quiet when I say for you to be quiet. There will be others along with us and I'll not have you jeopardize their safety in any way. Promise?"

"I promise," Marla said. "And thank you."

Les grunted. They said a fool was born every day; he knew of at least one who had been born on his birthday. If Sheriff Carl Wall ever got back from that fancy honeymoon trip of his, Les was going to ask him how a lawman handled stubborn women.

His only hope was that once Marla got a good look at the horses they would have to ride she would change her mind about going with him.

Marla reminded herself that Mary had been forced to ride a donkey to get where she needed to go. Then Marla looked at the defiant glint in the eye of the horse looking at her from across the barn and she wondered if a donkey wouldn't be easier to handle.

Marla was with Les and Elmer at the Redfern barn and Chrissy was showing them the two horses that could make a ride tonight. It was a little before midnight, but Chrissy had been expecting them because of Les's call. She looked too young to be the mother of two children, one a three-year-old son. She had on an old sweatshirt and sweatpants, and her blond hair was pulled back and tied with a scarf.

The Redferns' barn was smaller than the one Les had, and Marla thought it looked more like what she imagined that manger scene with Mary and Joseph would be like. For one thing, there were more kinds of animals around. But that might be only because there were chickens nesting on a tall shelf in one of the horse stalls, and once they had been woken up, they kept squawking until it seemed as if there were a lot of animals besides the cows and horses in the poorly lit barn.

"You can borrow my boots," Chrissy suggested to Marla. "If they're too big, I have lots of thick socks."

"Thank you." Marla wondered why Montana people had such a fascination with their socks.

Chrissy was still looking at her critically. "And I have a wraparound scarf, too. That will keep your face warm."

Marla looked over at where Les and Elmer were talking. They were stroking the heads of the two horses while they whispered together about something.

"I don't want to hold them up." Marla jerked her head at the men. "I'll do fine with what I have on."

"It'll only take me a minute to get them," Chrissy said as she started walking to the barn door. "Besides, they have to wait for the guys to get here from the Elkton ranch, anyway."

Marla nodded. Of course they needed to wait. There were only two horses at the Redfern place and with Les, Elmer and her, they would need three horses. Marla looked at the two disgruntled horses standing beside the men now. She hoped she was the one who got the other horse that would be coming. She would guess that Mary's donkey had been grateful for the privilege of carrying her around on its back; those two horses looked as if they'd just as soon stay in their warm stalls for the night and not be bothered with doing anything for anyone.

Marla changed her mind about the horses

when the Elkton men called to them from outside the barn. She went to the door and looked out. Some of those horses looked fierce. One was stomping his feet impatiently and another was blowing into the air. They looked as if they were ready to go into battle. She wondered why no one rode donkeys anymore.

"Is that all?" Les asked from where he stood just outside the barn door. "Don't you have another horse?"

Marla was glad Les recognized that none of the horses she'd seen tonight was suitable for her. She'd never been on a horse before; she needed a gentle ride.

There was a yard light that illuminated the area by the barn, and eight men with horses stood there waiting. The men all had heavy coats on their backs and boots on their feet. They all had Stetson hats on their heads, too, and when Marla looked more closely, she saw that they had knit scarves under their hats. It looked as if the hats held the scarves in place.

When the men heard Les's question, they looked at each other.

"Didn't Byron say he'd do that?" one of the men finally muttered.

Marla looked again. She did recognize Byron, the man from church on Sunday.

"Weren't you supposed to bring the other horse?" another man finally said directly to Byron.

Marla saw Byron shrug. "I figured she'd rather ride with someone, since I doubt she even knows how to ride. I thought I'd let her ride with me."

Les looked at Marla suspiciously. "You never said anything about not being able to ride a horse."

"Maybe I can ride," Marla said.

"I should have known." Les shook his head. "Well, that settles it—you have to stay here. We don't have a horse for you, anyway."

"I can ride with someone."

"She's welcome to ride with me," Byron said as he walked his horse closer to the barn door. He smiled down at Marla. "I always have room for a lady to ride with me."

Les groaned. "She's riding with me. Let's get going."

Marla thought it might be safer to ride with Byron. Les was looking even more disgruntled than the horses did. "I don't mind riding with Byron."

Les glared at her. "You're riding with me."

Marla followed Les over to the horse he had for the night. Chrissy had already said that one was named Stubby for stubborn. She reached out her hand and lightly touched the horse's side.

"You don't need to be frightened," Les said softly as he came up beside her.

"I've never touched a horse before."

Les smiled briefly. "I figured that."

Les put one of his feet in the stirrup and swung himself into the saddle.

Then he reached down for Marla's hand and moved his foot out of the stirrup. "Put your left foot there and swing up when I say."

Marla took his arm and put her foot in the stirrup.

"Now."

"Oh." Just like that, Marla was on the back of a horse.

"You okay?"

"I think so." Marla squirmed a little. She had not thought the horse's back would be quite so wide.

"Good. Move in as close as you can and hold on to me."

Marla didn't want to get too close, so she settled in with a couple of inches between her front and Les's back. And then the horse took a step forward and she plastered herself to his back. How did anyone ever stay seated on these things? Weren't they supposed to be as comfortable as rocking chairs?

Les had taken the horse outside the barn to join the other riders. It wasn't until everyone stood in the security light in the yard that Marla noticed every saddle except the one on Les's horse also had a long leather pocket. Out of that pocket stood a rifle.

Marla shivered, and it had nothing to do with the cold night air or the fact that she was riding on an animal that could, at any minute, rid himself of her. What chance did the night have with so many rifles around?

"God bless you," Chrissy called softly as the horsemen all started to file past the barn.

Marla smiled at Chrissy and waved. She would have felt better if Mrs. Hargrove had been here to pray for everyone. She could only hope that, wherever the older woman was, she was praying.

The night had a scattering of distant stars and she could see the subtle shift in the sky from black to deep gray that signaled there were clouds above them.

"Here," Les said, and Marla felt him reach back toward her with something. She took it in her hand. It was a soft wool scarf like the ones the other men had around their necks. "Put it on. It's going to be snowing any minute now."

Marla wrapped the scarf around her head and rested her cheek against Les's back. He was wearing a heavy wool jacket, and if she leaned her cheek against the black jacket for a couple of minutes the wool became warm. With the scarf wrapped around her and her face pressed to the warm space on Les's back, she was almost cozy in all this darkness.

She saw her first snowflake. It settled on Les's jacket near her face, glistening for a moment before her breath made it melt. The air felt moist and smelled damp. She could feel the pull of Les's arm muscles through his jacket as he used the reins to guide the horse.

Les was at the head of the line of horsemen. No one spoke. The only sounds were the horse hooves scraping the ground. They rode down a ravine until they reached a barbed-wire fence.

"Go ahead and cut it," Les said to another man who had stepped down from his horse. "I don't have cattle in this pasture right now, anyway."

The horsemen bunched up together as they waited for the fence to be cut.

"You doing okay?" a man leaned in and asked Marla.

With his hat pulled over his face, it took Marla a second to recognize Byron. She smiled at him. "Yes. Thanks for asking."

"If you need any help, let me know."

"She's fine," Les interrupted with a look over his shoulder at the other man.

When the fence was cut, the horses started to move again. Marla felt the cold on her legs above the line of the boots she had borrowed from Chrissy and on the back of her head where the wool scarf did not reach.

Les shifted in the saddle and Marla shifted with him. She wondered if Mary had ever ridden behind Joseph's back on that donkey. She hoped for the young girl's sake that she had. Despite the problems Marla knew would face them all when they reached the barn, she felt safe riding behind Les.

Chapter Thirteen

Les put his hand up and everyone pulled their horses to a stop. They had ridden up to the edge of the ravine surrounding the buildings on his ranch. The sheriff's department from Miles City should have had time to get themselves in place by now. Not that they would be close enough to do much if everything fell apart. The only place for them to wait, and not be seen, was well back of the last rise before the dip that led down to his buildings.

The night was still dark, but the light layer of snow that had been falling would make them all stand out more as they approached the house and barn. They would need to be especially quiet.

Les leaned back a little so he could feel Marla's warmth against him. He was going to have to find her a place to stay where she would be out of any trouble that might start. Probably the best thing would be to have her stay with the horses.

Les scanned the buildings. There was a sub-dued light coming from the window in the back of his barn. It was from the section that was now the workshop. He never kept a light burning when he left the workshop. Sometimes he used a night-light in the barn during calving season, but at this time of year there was no need for a light.

"Someone's there, all right," Elmer whispered as he rode up beside Les.

Les nodded. He had already noted that as they rode around the edge of the rise to the place that dipped down behind his buildings, he could see the front windows to the barn and no light was showing through them. Since there was a light in the back window, that meant whoever was inside had covered the windows in front. The road into his place looked squarely at those front windows. Which could only mean that whoever was inside his barn was trying to hide the fact that they were in his workshop. They would not expect anyone to see the window in the back.

Les wondered briefly if they were planning to catch him unaware or if they were hoping he just wouldn't check the barn when he got back home tonight.

"We'll leave the horses behind the house," Les whispered to the other men as he touched the flank of his horse to urge him to keep going down the slight hill. The snow made the ground slippery and the horses had to pick their way down.

Someone listening closely could have heard the sounds of hooves sliding across small rocks. The person would have to be outside, though, and Les was betting that none of the young men in his barn would want to linger outside on a night as cold as this one. And they had no reason to be outside. They were no doubt inside waiting for the sound of his pickup and the glare of his headlights coming from the opposite direction.

It took twenty minutes to ride from the top of the rise to the flat area in back of Les's house.

Les was relieved they had made it to the house without anyone inside the barn looking out that back window. He hadn't expected them to look and wasn't sure that they would see anything, anyway, since their eyes would not be accustomed to the dark. All they might have seen was a shadowy shape. An old mountain man would know to investigate something like that. Young men from the city wouldn't give it a second thought.

Les dismounted, then lifted his arms up to Marla. She practically fell into his arms, and he held her steady for a minute when her feet touched the ground.

"Cold?" he asked.

Marla nodded. "Sore, too."

"Maybe you should sit here and rest." Les had been trying to figure out how to convince Marla she needed to stay somewhere safe, and had concluded that his best plan would be to not tell her it was for her safety. "We need someone to stay with the horses."

"Stay with the horses! I don't know anything about horses."

Marla's voice had gotten a little high.

"Hush," Les said in a soft whisper. "We don't want anyone to hear us."

No sooner had the words left his mouth than Les wondered if Marla would like the young men inside the barn to hear them. He probably should have gagged her at some point tonight before they got this close.

He wasn't sure he could have done it even if he had thought of it, though. Les told himself that when the regular sheriff got back to

Dry Creek, he was going to turn in his reserve deputy sheriff badge. He'd let someone else go around putting gags on people.

"You're not going to make lots of noise and warn them, are you?" Les asked.

The night had gotten even darker than when they'd started out and Les could not see Marla's face clearly. Of course, with the scarf wrapped around it, he wouldn't have been able to see much of it even if it had been a full sunny day. He still had his hands on her arms to steady her, though, and he could feel her muscles tighten in indignation.

"All I want is for everyone to be safe," she said.

Les nodded. "That's why we don't want to give them a chance to use that rifle. Which means no noise."

"I understand that."

"Good."

Les looked around. He wished he hadn't kept the area around his house so tidy. There was nothing to tie the horses to. He'd even taken out the old clothesline when the posts started to rot. Since he didn't need the line, he'd never replaced it. He had an old lawn chair where he sat in the summer and looked at the wildflowers that grew all the way up the rise, but that wasn't enough to keep a horse from straying.

"You'll have to hold the reins," Les finally said as he turned to Marla. He couldn't spend all night looking for somewhere to anchor the reins.

"For all the horses?"

Les nodded, then looked at the men in front of him. "Elmer, maybe you could?"

"I'll stay with her," the older man said. "But if I hear trouble, I'm going to let these horses fend for themselves and come help."

Les nodded. "Thanks."

"Where shall we go in?" one of the Elkton ranch hands asked as he unsnapped the scabbard holding his rifle. He drew the long Winchester out and cradled it next to his shoulder.

"I figure we'll circle the barn. A man at each window. Don't worry about breaking the windows. Just don't do it until they know we're there." Les took the rifle Elmer handed to him.

"Everybody loaded?" Les asked as he cracked the rifle he'd just been given and made sure there were bullets in it. He knew the Elkton ranch hands took their rifles when they went into the far pastures on horseback, just in case they ran into wolves or maybe even a mountain lion if they were high enough in the hills.

Les saw a series of Stetsons nod.

"Well, then," he said, his voice still low, "I'll go around by the entrance and see if I can make sense of what's happening inside. Remember, we want to avoid any gunplay."

Les saw Marla wince.

"We plan to do this quietly," Les added for good measure. "Everyone take their station by a window, but wait until we figure out what's happening inside. Those boys might just be hanging out and happy to give up the rifle and come out peacefully."

"Maybe they didn't even take the rifle," Marla whispered.

Les nodded. "That's possible, too."

He supposed it was *possible*, Les told himself. In the realm of what was possible, maybe Mrs. Hargrove had stolen it. Or Linda, at the café. Or Santa Claus. Still, he couldn't say no to the hope that sprang up in Marla's mind.

When Les had talked to the sheriff in Miles City, they had gone over strategies. They had decided not to use a bullhorn and call out to the young men inside until Les could figure out where Sammy stood on all of this. Les didn't want to risk anyone making Sammy their hostage just in case he hadn't gone with the other men willingly.

It was a small chance that Sammy was innocent, but Les wanted to give him every benefit of the doubt even if it made his own job tonight more dangerous.

"It wouldn't hurt to say a prayer before we head out," Les added.

To a man, the ranch hands bowed their heads.

After they prayed, they each gave their reins to Elmer and followed Les over to the barn.

Marla watched as the men walked away. She could see dark shadows as they moved toward the barn. A snowflake fell on her eyelash and she blinked it away so she could see better. The men looked so powerful walking in the dark with their rifles resting against their shoulders and pointing to the sky. Each man walked differently. All of them were wearing tall leather boots, though, and she could hear the muffled sounds of their boot heels hitting rocks here and there.

"They should have bulletproof vests," Marla whispered.

Elmer grunted in response. "Don't worry about that boy of yours. Les will take care of him."

Marla didn't say that she'd meant Les was the one who should have the bulletproof vest. She supposed it was expecting too much for the Dry Creek people to forgive her and Sammy this time around. It was one thing for Sammy to steal the church's shepherd; it was another for him to help steal the sheriff's rifle. She looked over at Elmer. The older man had changed out of the suit he had worn earlier this evening. If he had been willing to play the harp because he thought Les was going to propose to someone, Elmer would probably take Les's point of view on anything.

Which was as it should be, Marla thought to herself. Les belonged here; it was good that his friends stood beside him. She might wish that they were her friends, too, but one look at Elmer's face and she knew it wasn't true. He didn't trust her, either.

When this night was over, Marla thought to herself, she would have to start packing again. She had to believe Sammy was innocent in all that was happening tonight, but even if he was innocent, their days of being welcome in Dry Creek were likely over. Her neighbor from Los Angeles had been right. People in small towns didn't like having gang members show up in their towns. Not that she could blame them,

Marla thought. She didn't like the gang showing up in her family, either.

Les put his hand against the front of the barn.
The old boards were dry from many years of
sun and wind, but he kept them painted, and
a few years ago he'd had the boards all sanded
down. He had taken off his gloves to give them
to Marla and now the wet snow on the barn
chilled his fingers. He looked up and could
see a couple of the Elkton men ahead of him,
each stationed at one of the windows in the
front of the barn.

The windows had been an extravagance a
decade ago when Les had them installed. He
liked to have the extra sunlight for the calves.
He'd never thought he would be using them
to help disarm some big-city gang members.

Les inched toward the smallest door that
led into the barn. He had a huge cattle door
on one end of the barn that he could open if
he needed to, but there was a smaller door he
could use, as well. He knew there was some
risk in opening even the small door, but there
was no other way, outside of looking through
a window, to see what was happening inside
the barn. He didn't want to use a window because that made a man too vulnerable. If the

gang members inside were watching anything, they would be watching the windows, waiting to see headlights as a pickup came down the same drive they had used.

Les stopped close to the door. He could see the single tracks of what looked like two motorcycles. They must have driven them inside his barn for the night. If he hadn't seen the light from the back window, he wouldn't have a clue that someone was in his barn tonight.

It was just too bad there wasn't a way to see everything better. Suddenly Les realized that there was a way. Permanently braced against the barn was a ladder that led up to the hayloft. If he could get up there, he could look through some of those cracks in the floor of the loft and look right down into the barn and the workshop both. The last place anyone would be looking would be at the ceiling.

Les walked by several Elkton men and whispered his plan to go up to the hayloft.

The ladder was sturdy and, with his rifle strapped over his shoulder, Les was able to make the climb to the loft quietly. The hayloft was open all year around and Les only had to swing himself onto the floor when he reached that opening. There were old straw bales lying around and straw dust everywhere. The wind had blown some snow in tonight and the bales were wet to the touch when Les leaned on several of them. It was darker inside the loft than it had been outside and he waited for his eyes to adjust.

Les carefully walked on the floorboards. He knew if he stayed close to the stacks of bales, his extra weight would not be enough to make the boards creak. When he got to a good-sized crack, he knelt and put his eye to the space.

The two strangers were there, all right. One of them was sitting on the worktable and the other had pulled in a wooden stool Les kept near the stalls. They weren't doing anything. The drawers in his workshop had all been pulled out and the contents dumped on the worktable already, so they must have finished searching for things. They had the rifle. It was lying on the floor by the man sitting on the stool. An opened box of bullets was next to it, so Les assumed they had loaded the gun earlier.

As Les looked more closely, he revised his opinion that these were men. Linda had said she estimated the two strangers at being around seventeen, but Les had figured they were probably a year or two older. Seeing them now, though, he wondered if they were a year or two younger. They were really teenagers instead of men.

The one sitting on the worktable had tattoos covering his arms and he was holding a hammer in one hand, swinging it softly. Les looked at the other teenager, too. Neither one was wearing a coat. They looked cold.

Maybe they'd be glad to give up their adventure.

Les had to move to his left and look through another crack before he saw Sammy. His heart was glad when he saw that Sammy was bound, both hands and feet, and lying in a corner of the workshop. Maybe Marla wasn't the only one who had kept hoping that her son was a victim instead of participant in all of this. Sammy had a bruise on his face, but other than that he looked all right.

Les moved his hand to prepare to stand and felt some small pieces of straw move with him. His hand was wet and that's what had made the straw stick. Unfortunately, the straw that didn't stick was also lifted and it was now slipping through the crack he'd been looking through.

Les held his breath as he watched the straw float down to where the boys were. He'd have to wait for their attention to move to something else before he dared to lift himself up from the floor.

Sammy was the only one to look up. He gave a half grunt of surprise and then closed his mouth.

"What'ja doing now?" the guy with the hammer demanded of Sammy. "Didn't I just tell you to shut up?"

"Maybe he wants you to hit that shepherd of his again," the guy sitting on the stool said with a sneer. "Teach him to keep quiet. We're hiding out here. We don't need any little kid whining."

"Ah, ain't nobody coming out here tonight," the guy with the hammer answered. "It's snowing out there. The cops will all be someplace drinking coffee."

"Still, he should be quiet."

"Well, if it makes you feel better, here." The guy swung the hammer and hit the shepherd.

Les winced. No amount of putty was going to fix that Nativity figure now.

"You're going to be sorry you did that," Sammy growled as he struggled with the ties around his feet. "When I get my hands free, I'm going to—"

Both of the guys laughed.

"Yeah, you and who else are going to come

get us? You got any *amigos* around here that'll help you whip us?"

Sammy was quiet for a moment. Then he started to talk, low and fierce. "Yeah, I do. That shepherd belongs to God. You mess with His shepherd and He'll take your guts and grind them up until you'll wish you were dead. And then He'll have the buzzards come and drop you in the fire pit. And then—"

"Whoa—hey, man," the guy with the hammer said. Les thought he looked a little nervous. "I get your point."

"No disrespect to your God," the other one said.

"Well…" Sammy hesitated. "He's not my God, but I know a woman, Mrs. Hargrove, and—"

"Your *amigo* is a *woman*? So is she sexy?"

"Mrs. Hargrove? No way. She's old."

"Your *amigo* is an *old woman*. And she's going to help you whip us?"

Both of the guys laughed a little.

Sammy nodded emphatically. "God does what she asks Him to do. He'll come and get you if she says she wants you to be gotten."

"You mean she puts out a curse? My grandmother used to know about curses. I don't want any curses around me. They can shrivel a guy up. Some guy my cousin knew died from a curse like that."

Les figured, with all the talking going on down there, it was a good time to make his move back to the ladder. He only hoped Sammy didn't scare the other two guys too much. He'd rather have them half-asleep than all wide-awake and spooked.

Les climbed down and walked along the side of the barn again. Now that he knew where everyone was located in the workshop, he knew he could open the large cattle door without anyone seeing it. He oiled the hinges on that door every fall and he knew it wouldn't make a sound as it slid open tonight. The guys inside the workshop might feel a sudden drop in temperature when the cold air came into the barn, but they wouldn't hear anything to make them suspicious.

After stopping to tell the men from the Elkton ranch what his plan was, Les walked over to the cattle door and swung it open. The door opened to the wide aisle that ran down the center of his barn. The workshop and the horse stalls were on one side of the aisle. The cattle stalls were on the other.

The horse inside the barn was the first animal to notice the cold air, and he gave a loud whinny of protest. A couple of chickens squawked as Les slipped into the barn and inched his way along the side of the workshop. He moved to the workshop window that faced the front of the barn. He'd already noticed it was closed. No one inside would be able to hear him.

When he reached the workshop door, Les pushed on it gently. Sammy was the only one facing the door and Les hoped that the boy wouldn't give anything away. Once he had the door open a crack, he could hear them talking inside. They were still on the subject of curses.

"What was that?" one of the gang members said. Les thought it sounded like the guy sitting on the stool. He was the one with the rifle lying on the floor beside him. "Did you hear that?"

"Ah, you're just spooked," the other guy said. "It was the horse out there making noise."

"No, it was after that."

"Then it was the chickens. Relax."

Les knew he hadn't made any noise. The two of them were just jumpy after all the talk about curses.

"There it is again," the nervous one said. "And it ain't no chickens. I'll bet it's the cops."

"We haven't even seen any headlights," the other one said.

"No, but they're here…"

Les was wondering if the guy somehow saw the backup team from Miles City up on the rise. He supposed if someone up there had turned on a flashlight or something they would be seen. Suddenly a rifle shot shattered the window of the workshop.

Les decided it was now or never.

"Put your hands up. You're surrounded," Les yelled. He didn't stand where they could see him, but they could sure hear him.

Les heard the sound of windows breaking all over the barn.

"We've got a hostage!" one of the boys screamed out. He was so young his voice ended in a high squeak.

"What you've got is trouble," Les yelled back. "Put the rifle down and come on out here with your hands in the air."

That's when Les heard the thunder coming. The first horse to come galloping into the barn was Stubby from the Redfern place. Then there were a couple of the Elkton horses. Then there was—

Marla! She was chasing the horses. Or rather, trying to catch them. She had a rope outstretched and was looking at the animals in panicked frustration.

"Get back!" Les yelled, but he wasn't sure she could hear him over the sounds of horse hooves.

The men from the Elkton ranch sure didn't hear him. They all had a fondness for their horses, and they were sliding into the barn to calm them down.

"Who's there?" the youngster with the rifle shouted from the broken window. He swung the rifle around as if he didn't know who to shoot first.

Les heard eight rifles cock at the same minute.

"What the—" The teenager with the rifle saw all the rifles pointing at him.

In one motion, the men from the Elkton ranch had swung onto the backs of their horses while keeping their rifles trained on the boy in the window.

"It's time to give it up," Les said smoothly as he walked toward the teenager. There were too many guns ready to fire for his comfort. "No need to make this harder than it is."

Les saw the gang member looking at the Elkton men. The ranch hands had their Stetsons pulled low and the collars of their sheepskin coats pulled high around their necks. They had one hand on their horses and the other steadying their long-barreled rifles, all aimed at the teenager standing in the broken window of the workshop.

"You don't want to get hurt," Les continued softly as he took a few more steps closer. "Give me the rifle."

"Who are you guys? Some kind of a posse?"

The teenager dropped his rifle through the workshop window and it fell to the floor in the barn.

"We have a right to be arrested by the cops." The other teenager spoke up from inside the workshop. "We have our rights. Nobody is going to string us up."

"Drop the hammer and come out here," Les said.

The boy dropped the hammer as if it was on fire. "I'm not armed. No one can shoot me. I demand police protection."

Les heard several cars coming to a stop outside his barn.

"I think that's your protection now," Les said as several deputy sheriffs came inside the barn.

The two youngsters saw the uniforms and would have run to the deputies if the horses hadn't been in their way.

Les decided he needed to make the aisle in his barn wider. Between the horses and the deputies and the chickens that had been spooked and were flapping around, there wasn't enough room for Marla to get through to the workshop where Sammy was.

"He's all right," he turned and yelled just in case she could hear him.

Les stepped inside the workshop and saw Sammy where he had been earlier.

"You are all right, aren't you?" he asked as he walked over and squatted beside Sammy.

"God got them, didn't He?"

Les nodded as he started to unknot the rope around Sammy's hands. "He sure did."

"I'm going to be a cowboy when I grow up," Sammy announced. "And get me a hat and a rifle."

"Oh, no, you don't," Marla said as she stepped into the workshop. "You won't have any kind of gun."

"Les?" Sammy looked up in appeal.

"Listen to your mother," Les said as he moved to the knot on Sammy's feet. "She knows what she's talking about."

Sammy wasn't the only one who should have listened to Marla, Les thought to himself. He should have listened and believed a little more in the innocence of her son. He was going to apologize, but before he could get any words out, Marla had hurried Sammy up and rushed him out of the workshop. Les thought it seemed a little bit as though she couldn't stand to be in the same room with him.

Chapter Fourteen

Marla wrapped the blanket tighter around Sammy. After talking to Les, the deputy sheriff from Miles City had asked her and Sammy if they'd like to ride home in one of their cars. She was sitting with Sammy in one car and the two teenagers were sitting in the other car. The men were all standing outside talking and remounting their horses. The dome light was on inside the car, so Marla didn't have any trouble picking out the various men, even though the men who had been riding horseback were all wearing hats. She knew Les because of his coat.

Marla thought she should be content. She had her son sitting next to her and he wasn't hurt or even pulling away from her. He was safe and, hopefully, he had learned his lesson. She should concentrate on that and not wonder

what could have been between her and Les if
he'd been able to trust her. Trust was very important. Maybe he still didn't trust her. He certainly hadn't seemed to want her to ride back
with him on his horse.

Marla turned her attention to Sammy.

"Hopefully, you learned not to give out your
address to people who shouldn't have it," she
said. "Those guys shouldn't have even known
how to find you up here."

"I didn't give them our address. They got it
from our old landlord."

"Ah," Marla said. "Well, I'll have to call
him."

"They told him they needed to send me back
my baseball."

"Well, he shouldn't have believed that." She
would think he would have been less gullible.
Maybe he was and they'd paid him for the address.

"But they did have my baseball with my
name on it and everything. More than one.
Every time I got a baseball, they took it from
me."

Marla blinked. How many times had this
gone on? "But why didn't you tell me?"

"You were busy with Dad."

"Ah," Marla said. She probably wouldn't

have paid any attention to a missing baseball in those days, anyway. She put her arm around Sammy's shoulder. "I'm sorry I wasn't paying enough attention back then."

Sammy shrugged. "It's okay. Dad wasn't there to play catch with me, anyway."

Marla pulled Sammy closer. "You still miss your dad, don't you?"

Sammy nodded.

"Well, we're going to spend more time to-gether. You, me and Becky."

Sammy looked up. "I wouldn't mind if we had other people around, too."

Marla held her breath.

"Like Mr. Morales," Sammy added. "He's a good guy. And Les isn't too bad. And I like Mrs. Hargrove. And the woman at the café who gave us those doughnuts."

Marla nodded. "There's lots of good people in Dry Creek."

Marla told herself she needed to postpone moving. She knew small towns could be unfor-giving, and she and her children had probably made the worst first impression they possibly could have. She did not expect the people of Dry Creek to want them to stay even when it became clear to them that Sammy hadn't taken the sheriff's rifle. They would still say he'd brought the wrong kind of people to their town, and they would be right. But not even the people of Dry Creek could get all that talking done overnight.

She'd have to give the kids a hint, but she could wait until after Christmas to start packing up their boxes. Maybe by then, Sammy and Becky would feel better about moving. She could even just move into Miles City, which wouldn't be far away—and they would be going to school there even if they lived in Dry Creek, so it might not make too much difference to them.

Yes, Miles City would be a good place to go. It would be a fresh start. Of course, she'd have to rent a place for them to live in Miles City. She wondered if someone would be willing to buy the house in Dry Creek.

Her mind was still trying to figure out how she'd pull off a move when the deputy sheriff came back to the car.

"Well, we've got it all wrapped up," he said as he slid into the driver's seat "Ready to head home?"

"Thank you, Deputy—?"

"Sutter, ma'am. Deputy Sutter," he said as he started the car.

"And you're from Miles City?"

"I sure am," he said with a grin in the rear-view mirror. "I've lived there my whole life."

"Well, then, you can tell us about it," Marla said.

Marla saw Sammy listen intently to the deputy talk about how the kids in town played softball in Bender Park and every year went to the rodeo called the Bucking Horse Sale.

"Can I ride in the rodeo?" Sammy demanded.

"Maybe someday," the deputy said. "But you have to grow taller first."

Sammy nodded. "I grow pretty fast."

Marla relaxed back into the seat as the deputy's car climbed up the slight hill leaving Les's place. Sammy would make the move to Miles City just fine. It made sense to move, anyway. There weren't very many other children for him to play with in Dry Creek. Miles City was a much bigger town. She was determined her children would have a fresh start and not have a negative reputation dogging their footsteps through their childhood.

When they got to the top of the rise, Marla looked back. All the lights were still on in Les's barn. She could even see the horses outlined in the light. She wondered if she'd ever see that barn or house again.

Les was standing by his barn, watching the taillights of the deputy's car as it drove away.

"Humph, so the great Lester Wilkerson is finally bitten," said a voice to his left.

Les didn't need to turn around to know who it was. "You should talk, Byron. You wine and dine them all."

Byron chuckled. "Maybe so. But you don't see me standing there looking like the dog someone left behind. All alone at home."

Les turned and looked at the man. "No, we don't see that, do we? Makes me wonder which one of us is the sorriest, though."

"Hey, don't take it out on me," Byron said as he raised his hands in surrender. "I'm on your side in all of this."

That fact made Les feel even worse. How had he ended up on the same side as Byron?

"Everybody's leaving," Les finally said. The truth was that the other riders had already gotten a couple of yards' head start on Byron. Les had promised them all a free piece of pie at the café the next time they were in town; he'd call Linda tomorrow and give her a deposit.

Byron took the hint and saddled up. "Remember, if you get lonesome, we've always got the coffeepot on in the bunkhouse in the winter."

"Thanks," Les said. There was a time when he'd enjoyed hanging out in the Elkton ranch bunkhouse. Maybe that time would come again. At the moment, though, all he wanted to do was go inside his house and sit.

The next day the Suzy bake set deluxe edition came in the mail for Les. He'd forgotten that the other night he'd ordered it online and checked the rush delivery box. Les had one of the ranches that were far enough outside Dry Creek to have actual mail delivery. Places that were close in were expected to pick up their mail at the hardware-store counter. Les had never been as grateful for the privacy of individual mail delivery as he was when he saw that box. He didn't want anyone to know he'd just gotten a Suzy bake set. Especially because he was suddenly unsure of what to do with it.

Oh, he knew he was going to give it to Becky. But should he just knock on the door to the Gossett house and hand it to her? He wasn't even sure he was still welcome there. And if he handed something to Becky, he had to have something for Sammy. It had occurred to Les sometime in the night that Sammy might have been leaving him those gang symbols as a warning.

If Sammy hadn't left them, Les wouldn't

even have known what he was up against. He owed the boy for that. So he definitely needed to get a present for Sammy. And, of course, if he gave something to the kids, shouldn't he give something to Marla?

It was a good thing, Les told himself, that he had his chores all done before the mail came, because he sure wasn't getting anything done after it was delivered. Finally he decided that if he was going to waste the day, anyway, he might as well drive into Miles City for supplies. If he happened to find a present for Sammy while he was there, so much the better.

The fact that he would have to drive through Dry Creek to go to Miles City was not important. Of course, as reserve deputy sheriff, he should check that the lights were still on in the Gossett place. He might even ask Linda at the café if anyone had seen the family today. After all, it was his duty to be sure that all the citizens of Dry Creek were safe.

Marla saw Les's pickup go by her house. She'd expected him to do his usual walk through Dry Creek this morning, but he hadn't. He'd stopped at the café, but then he just got back into his pickup and drove out of town. She had been waiting for him, too, because she'd realized last night when she got home that she still had the gloves he'd lent her. She wanted to return them.

She also realized she hadn't thanked him for untying Sammy last night. Her hands had been so cold she wouldn't have been able to do it. Of course, the fact that her hands were frozen was partially his fault. He'd left her to hold those horses' reins, and she hadn't been able to keep them straight with the gloves on, so she'd taken the gloves off.

She hoped she never had to see a horse again as long as she lived.

And she could have told Les all of that if he'd walked down the street so she could go out and talk to him.

Marla looked down the street. Maybe Linda knew when he was coming back. Maybe he was just going to do his walk a little later in the day because last night had been so, well, exciting.

It took Marla fifteen minutes to get a coat and mittens on Becky. Sammy had them both beaten. The children were anxious to go to the café—Marla had told them they could have a cup of cocoa. She decided they all needed to go out some. She hoped Linda would still treat them the same after all that had happened last night.

* * *

The cocoa was made with real milk. Marla couldn't remember the last time she'd had cocoa with real milk. She looked up at Linda. "This is great. Usually it's just from those packets."

"Growing kids need their milk," Linda said.

Marla tried to detect some difference in the way the café owner was treating them today. So far, she couldn't find any, but she had figured it would take the gossip and nervousness time to grow in Dry Creek, anyway. People hadn't had time to cluster together yet and decide they didn't want anyone in their town who might bring in gang people.

"I noticed the deputy sheriff didn't do his usual walk this morning," Marla finally said between sips. She kept looking at her cup so it would look as if she was only making an observation that anyone could make.

"He's going into Miles City to do some Christmas shopping," Linda said. "At least, that's what I'm assuming. He kept asking me what kind of present a young woman would want."

"Oh." Marla knew it was nothing to her if Les bought Linda a present. The two of them had known each other forever, in any event.

"I told him he had to listen for himself. Most women will say they want this or they want that. All a man has to do is pick one."

"Well, that's good advice." Marla sipped her cocoa. Linda was really a very nice young woman. If Les was looking in that direction, she would have to congratulate him on his good taste.

Not that he would have a quick courtship. Linda had been too supportive of Les when she thought he was going to propose to Marla to make anyone imagine the café owner was romantically inclined toward Les.

"I want a Suzy bake set," Becky announced as she set her empty cup down on the table.

"I have a cupcake pan at home I can give you," Marla said. "We can make cupcakes in that."

"I have a jar of Christmas sprinkles in the back," Linda offered. "You could make some pretty Christmas cupcakes."

Marla noticed the disappointment in Becky's eyes.

"They'll be grown-up cupcakes, then. Won't that be fun?" Marla said.

"Yes, Mommy."

"I'd like to see your cupcakes when you have

them all made," Linda said softly. "I bet they'll be beautiful."

Becky nodded.

Linda went into the kitchen and Marla set four dollars down on the table. She knew from the menu that a cup of cocoa was a dollar. She left the fourth dollar as a tip.

Linda gave Becky the bottle of sprinkles, then looked at the dollar bills. She gave three of them back to Marla. "There's a junior special on cocoa."

Marla frowned. "It doesn't say anything about that in your menu."

Linda waved her hand. "We never put our children's specials in the menu. We just tell people that come in with children. We don't want to make our regular customers feel bad."

"I see," Marla said. "But I'm not a child."

"Don't worry. I gave you all the junior special. It's my reward for you bringing in new business."

Marla looked at her.

Linda nodded cheerfully. "Children like yours will grow up to be my future customers."

"We'll come back," Sammy assured her as he set his empty cup on the table. "Even if we're moved to Miles City. We'll come back for cocoa."

"What?"

Marla blushed. "It's just that the children will be going to school in Miles City, anyway. And it'd be more convenient if we were there."

"And I broke the shepherd here," Sammy said as he wiped the cocoa off his face. "He's broken so bad even Les can't fix him."

"Well, yes, but it's only a plastic figure," Linda protested. "Surely you wouldn't move because of that."

"We're not doing anything before Christmas," Marla assured the woman as she stood. That would give the nervous ones in Dry Creek time to voice all the reasons why it would be just as well if the Gossett family did move someplace else. "And Sammy's right. We will still come back and say hello."

"Thanks for my sprinkles," Becky called as they walked toward the door.

"Yes, thanks for everything," Marla added as she opened the door.

The air outside was warmer than it had been yesterday and Marla kept a steady pace with the children as they crossed the street.

"There's where the shepherd should be." Sammy pointed to the Nativity set as they walked past the church. "Right there by those sheep of his."

"Les is taking care of the sheep," Becky said with a worried look on her face. She looked up at her mother. "Isn't he?"

"I'm sure he is, sweetheart."

Marla wondered how long her children would continue to think that Les could fix all the problems in the world.

Chapter Fifteen

Les looked at the presents on his table and wondered if he'd made a mistake. He'd wrapped Becky's Suzy bake set in red paper and the junior-size Stetson he'd gotten for Sammy in green paper. All the wrapping paper only made the pork loin roast for Marla look worse than it had when he'd started his wrapping, though.

Not that the roast looked bad. He'd talked to the butcher himself and gotten a prime piece of fresh meat.

It's just that he was starting to wonder if Linda's advice had been so good. She'd told him to buy something the woman in question had said she wanted, and the only thing he could remember Marla saying she wanted was a pork roast to use in her tamales. Looking at the roast, though, he was beginning to think he should have bought her a gold brooch instead. His mother had always liked a gold brooch for Christmas.

Of course, he hadn't noticed that Marla wore any jewelry, so she might not like any kind of a brooch, either. And jewelry meant a bigger thank-you than a roast. Les didn't want to make Marla feel uncomfortable with his presents.

He'd already caused her to have to sit through that circus at the café the other night when people thought he was going to propose. Les wanted to save her further scenes. He wanted her to know he intended to court her in a quiet, respectful manner. He didn't want her to think he was pushing her to make a decision.

After all, Les told himself, he couldn't expect her to have the same certainty that he felt about them getting together. He'd always been someone who knew right away what he wanted. It could be because he'd seen his parents bend and sway so much over the years. Whatever it was, he knew he wanted to have Marla at his side in his life. So the first Christmas present was important.

Maybe it was too soon to even give a present, though.

In fact, Les told himself as he unwrapped Sammy's hat, he should just let the items sit in the big box they were in and not even make them into presents. He'd just leave the box on the steps of the house tonight, without his name on it. That way, no one needed to worry about whether the present was too little or too big. And no one would need to thank anyone.

Les was relieved he'd finally figured out what to do. It was cold enough that he wouldn't need to worry about refrigerating the roast. If he got up and drove into Dry Creek before he did his morning chores, the box would be on Marla's doorstep when she woke up.

And he'd have the joy of giving a merry Christmas to her and her kids without anyone feeling awkward, including himself. Les looked at the box again. It looked a little drab. Maybe he should stuff some of the wrapping paper in the corners of the box. Sort of fluff the whole thing out.

He could just picture Marla getting the box in the morning. She'd be pleased. Just picturing her face was reward enough for him. He didn't need some big thank-you.

Marla was furious. She'd just opened the door this morning, and what did she see? A charity box. Her family had received enough of those when she was a child that she recognized all the characteristics. The toys for the children weren't wrapped, but there was wrapping paper placed in the box so the parents could do it. As though that made the presents actually come from the parents. And of course, there was the ever-present large food item. At least someone in the church had had some cultural sensitivity and had given her pork for her tamales instead of a turkey.

Marla almost sat down and cried. She had lived all those years in Los Angeles and never been reduced to being the target of a charity box. At least in Los Angeles they asked a family if they wanted a box. A family had to sign up on a list or wait in some line. Here in Dry Creek, everyone just assumed her family was the poorest family around.

She resisted the urge to go out onto the street and see if there were boxes on any other porches. She knew there wouldn't be.

And the worst part was, Marla thought, she was going to accept the box. It was only three days until Christmas. The refund check hadn't come yet. How else would she get a Suzy bake set for Becky and a cowboy hat for Sammy? She couldn't deny them those presents, not

even if it cost her all her pride to keep them.
She just wished there was something she could
do to show people that she wasn't the desperate charity case everyone apparently assumed
she was.

Marla fretted for an hour before the idea
came to her. If it was more blessed to give than
to receive, then she just needed to out-give the
church people to regain some of her pride. Of
course, she didn't have money to give anyone.
But now that she had the pork roast, she could
have lots and lots of tamales.

Maybe—and this thought brought a smile to
her face—she would give a tamale to anyone
in Dry Creek who wanted one. She didn't quite
know how to go about presenting her gift, but
Mrs. Hargrove would know.

The next morning Les sat in the café drinking his second cup of coffee and scowling at
the frost on the windows.

"Calf sick?" Linda asked as she quietly re-
filled his coffee cup.

"No, why?"

Linda shrugged. "I've just never seen you
this worried before. I figured it must be something wrong at your place."

Les sighed. "No, my place is fine."

Linda set her coffeepot on the table and sat in the chair opposite Les.

"Then what's wrong? Anything I can help with?"

Les snorted. "You've already helped enough."

"Me? What did I do?"

Les caught himself. "Sorry. I should have just thanked you for your advice and let it be. No one forced me to take the advice."

"This is about that present?"

Les nodded. "I got her what she said she wanted, but now I'm wondering if it's the right thing."

Linda smiled. "I've never seen you this worked up over a present before. Anyone I know?"

"It's none of your business." Les did his best to glare at Linda. He didn't need gossip going around about him and some present. His heart wasn't really in the glare, though. He had other problems to trouble him.

"Well, if you don't think that what this mystery woman said she wanted is what she really wants, then at least get her something that she needs," Linda said. "You can't go too far off base when you get someone what they need."

Les set down his coffee cup and grinned at her. "I should have thought of that before."

"Good. I'm glad that's solved." Linda stood up. "Do you want me to keep your coffee hot for when you finish your walk around town?"

Les shook his head. "I don't have time to walk this morning. I've got to go back into Miles City."

He needed to buy someone a pair of thick socks. Marla was probably the only one in Dry Creek who didn't own any winter socks. She'd probably like that better than that pork roast, anyway. And she needed them.

His problems were solved.

Marla knew Les was having his cup of coffee in the café. She had seen his pickup parked outside and she'd put on her jacket so that when he walked down the street past her house, she could go out and thank him for what he'd done for Sammy. She owed him her thanks and she meant to say as much to him.

She was trying not to be obvious about looking out her front window, but she did notice when he stepped outside the café and stood on the porch. He wore his bulky black jacket and Marla remembered, just for a moment, how the wool had felt against her cheek in the cold. She wasn't sure anymore if it was the wool or the solid weight of Les himself that she'd found so comforting that night. She should thank him for letting her go with him then, though, as well as for what he'd done for Sammy.

Les took a long look down the street in both directions and then walked right back to his pickup. He opened the door, got inside, then drove through town just as he had yesterday.

In all the time Marla had been in Dry Creek, the one thing that had happened every day, rain or shine, was that Reserve Deputy Sheriff Wilkerson did a morning patrol down the street. She'd never seen him find any problems on his morning walk, but he faithfully made it nonetheless.

Until now. Marla felt herself grow cold, and she had a fire already going in the fireplace. It suddenly hit her that the only reason Les would stop making his morning patrol was that he was avoiding someone. And that someone could only be her and her family. Who else had given Les Wilkerson any trouble lately?

Marla walked over and sat on a folding chair. She put her elbows on the table and just sat there. She had thought Les was becoming attached to her and her family, but it wouldn't be the first time she hadn't been able to read a man's heart right. If she hadn't known her own husband was being unfaithful, how could she expect to know the intentions of a man she'd met for the first time a little over a week ago?

At least she hadn't made a fool of herself over him. She had her dignity, at least. And she and the children would be moving after Christmas, anyway. Oh—the children. What would she tell the children about Les? Sammy had asked about the man yesterday, and Marla had said he was probably busy. She wasn't sure how long that answer would satisfy her son.

Les was the first man Sammy had attached himself to since his father had died. Maybe Sammy would be content to see Les in church. She was sure the man would attend the Christmas Eve service, and that was only two days away. He would have to be friendly to Sammy in church. There had to be rules in the Bible about that.

Thoughts of the Christmas Eve service reminded Marla that she had a lot to do before then. She'd talked to Mrs. Hargrove yesterday and the older woman had been delighted with Marla's idea of serving up sweet pork tamales after the Christmas carols were sung around the Nativity scene.

Which meant, Marla told herself, that she would need to get busy. She would show the town of Dry Creek that she and her children weren't charity cases if it was the last thing she did before leaving town.

Thinking of leaving town reminded Marla that she needed to ask Linda if the café had some empty boxes they were planning to throw away. Marla had already burned all the boxes she had packed for their trip up here. She hadn't planned that they would ever move again, and the boxes made good starter material for the fireplace. She'd used the last piece of cardboard for the fire this morning.

She'd miss the fireplace, too. Last night she and the children had roasted hot dogs for dinner. Maybe in their new place in Miles City, they would have a fireplace.

Les sat at his kitchen table again. He'd finished his evening chores and he was looking at the presents he'd bought today in Miles City. What had looked so practical in the bright afternoon sun in Miles City was now looking a little disorganized in the unforgiving glare of his overhead light. He looked around his kitchen as though there would be a solution to his problem, but there wasn't.

He'd just have to make the best of it. Les had found some thick wool socks for Marla at one store in Miles City, then he'd remembered Sammy and Becky. They would need thick socks this winter, too. So instead of the neat pair of socks he'd first envisioned, he had a jumble of socks. He had, of course, realized that one pair of socks wouldn't be enough for any of them. So he'd gotten ten pairs for each of them.

And now he didn't know if he should just put them all in a box together or if he should divide them so it was obvious there were three types of socks. He supposed the socks he'd gotten for Becky would be easy enough to identify. He confessed he'd gotten a little carried away with Becky's socks. He hadn't even known they had socks for little girls that had ballerinas on them. And the princess socks. Of course, they weren't thick, but how could he not buy those? He could have passed on the mermaid socks, but they were blue and the T-shirt Becky had worn the other day was blue.

Fortunately, Sammy's socks were easy to buy. White, extra-thick athletic socks were what he needed, especially for gym class at school.

Les had been a little uncomfortable buying Marla's socks. He'd had no idea that women's socks were so much softer than the ones men bought. He'd been rubbing his fingers over a pair of socks when the saleslady had come over and asked if he needed help. He'd quickly bought ten pairs of socks, in various pastel colors, just because he didn't want the woman to think he had a sock problem or anything.

Marla woke up the day before Christmas Eve and looked at the wooden cross that hung on the wall opposite where she rolled out her sleeping bag each night. The one thing she needed to do before she moved to Miles City was talk to Mrs. Hargrove about that cross. Maybe the older woman would be able to tell her what her husband had gained from it.

The sun was just beginning to rise as Marla walked through the house for the first time that day. She didn't even bother to look out her window to see if Les was going to make his patrol. In fact, she was going to leave the blankets on the windows until it was past the time when he usually made a patrol. That should let him know she wasn't waiting around to see if he would walk down the street. And even if she had been watching in the past couple of days, it was only because she still had Les's gloves and she needed to return them to him.

Marla was making tamales today, with the help of Sammy and Becky, and she was too busy to watch the street traffic, anyway. She was looking forward to sharing her tamales with the people of Dry Creek tomorrow night at the Christmas Eve service.

Les got the word from Elmer who had talked to Mrs. Hargrove who had talked to Linda. He couldn't believe it, though. Marla and the kids were moving! Because Sammy had taken the Nativity shepherd.

"I thought all that about the shepherd had been settled," Les said to Linda as he marched into the café. "That's no reason for anyone to leave town. The first time Sammy damaged the shepherd it was an accident and the second time it wasn't even him doing it."

"Don't tell me about it. I agree with you," Linda said as she finished setting silverware on one of the tables.

It was midafternoon and no one else was in the café.

"You're sure that's what Marla said?" Les asked.

"Ask her yourself if you don't trust me. She even came in here asking for boxes."

"But she's making her tamales for everyone for tomorrow night."

Les knew the tamales were important to

Marla and that's why he hadn't gone over there and bothered her. He figured tomorrow night was soon enough to wish her a Merry Christmas.

"I think they're her goodbye present to us all."

"Well, I won't eat one, then. I'm not saying goodbye."

Linda looked at him. "Have you told her how you feel? Maybe that would make a difference."

"It's too soon to say how I feel," Les said. He sat down at a table. He was one miserable person. "She'll think it's all just a come-on if I start babbling about how much I'd miss her and how I think her hair is beautiful and that she's the perfect woman for me."

"I could vouch for you. I could tell her you've never said anything like that to another woman."

Les looked at her. "How do you know?"

Linda smiled. "You're a legend of sorts around here, Lester Wilkerson. You and Byron. Him for saying everything to everyone and you for not saying anything to anyone. Ever. We women talk, you know."

"Well, I'm a quiet man," Les admitted.

"Tell me something I don't know."

There was a moment's silence. "I did write a poem about how her hair reminded me of Mrs. Hargrove's coffee. I could recite that to her."

Linda looked at him dubiously. "Maybe you could sing her a song instead. You've got a good singing voice and there's got to be a thousand love songs around."

"But would she listen to me sing her a song? She wasn't very happy with me when we had to go after Sammy."

"Well, I…" Linda's voice started off confidently and then trailed off. "You haven't talked to her since that night?"

Les shook his head. "I know I should have trusted her to know her own son. Instead, I got all carried away thinking she might be dealing drugs or something herself."

"Marla? Oh, she's not the type."

Les nodded miserably. "And if you could see that, do you think she'll forgive me for not seeing it?"

Linda hesitated and put her hand on his arm. "I hope so."

"Maybe if I could fix that old shepherd up, she wouldn't feel like she and the kids had to move."

"Mrs. Hargrove said something about replacing that shepherd, too. I think she's working on some idea."

"I'll eat more soup. Just sign me up."

"You know, maybe I could make a shepherd, too," Linda said.

Les stood up. He had work to do if he expected to get that shepherd in a kneeling position again.

Chapter Sixteen

Christmas Eve turned out to be a clear night. When Marla looked straight up, she could see stars. She wished one of them was as bright as the one the wise men had followed, but she was happy to see the lesser stars sprinkled across the dark sky, anyway. Not every star could be the brightest one. She knew that in her own life.

Marla had packed a hundred foil-wrapped tamales and Sammy was pulling them along in an old play wagon that had been behind their house when they moved there. Marla thought her husband's uncle had probably used it to pull wood in for the fireplace. The wagon was a little lopsided, but she and the children were walking slowly and the wagon kept up.

Marla wondered if anyone in the church would be struck by the irony that she had packed the tamales in the same box that had been left on her doorstep with the children's presents and the pork roast. She certainly hoped so, because she'd gotten another charity box this morning. This one had no name, either, and it was filled with socks. Usually charity boxes had socks and mittens, but this one had just socks. Not that she was complaining. The socks were wonderful, soft and pretty. If whatever group who left the sock box had also left a card saying who the box was from, she might have been able to convince herself it was a present. But if a gift like that was anonymous, it was a charity box.

She couldn't live in a town that pitied her. She felt a little sad walking down the street toward the church with her children at her side. This evening would probably be their last celebration in the little town.

It was best that they moved to Miles City. She owed Sammy and Becky a hometown that would respect them.

Marla could already hear the people talking. The porch light was on at the church and people were gathered around the Nativity set at the foot of the outside stairs. The only figure in the Nativity that she could see was the angel. It hung from the rain gutters of the church proclaiming good news for everyone.

Marla looked down to be sure Becky was keeping up.

She smiled at her daughter. No matter where they lived, all was well.

Marla had had a long discussion with Mrs. Hargrove yesterday about the wooden cross, and she knew a lot more now about religious symbols. Her husband had not really been getting any answers from that cross; he was probably just remembering what he knew of the Bible when he looked up at it. Mrs. Hargrove told her she could have the same insights. She planned to meet with Mrs. Hargrove next week again to talk about it.

"Look," Sammy said as he stopped the wagon.

Marla looked up. "Oh."

The people had parted so that the three of them could see the full Nativity scene.

"They've got shepherds," Sammy shouted.

Marla didn't even tell him that one shouldn't shout in church. She couldn't believe what she saw, either. Right there, where the shepherd should be but wasn't, there were four other shepherd figures. Even though none of them lit up like the original shepherd, there were

so many shepherds that the sheep were out-
numbered.

Sammy left the wagon where it was and ran
to the Nativity set. She saw Les bend down to
talk to him.

This was a picture Marla knew she would
never forget.

And then she saw Sammy walk behind one
of the shepherds, and the whole thing lit up
with white Christmas lights. Someone had
made a luminary in the shape of a shepherd.
Or, rather, it was a hundred luminaries grouped
together to make a shepherd.

The luminaries were as much a Hispanic tra-
dition as the tamales were, even if these luminaries were made from aluminum cans instead
of paper bags. There were Christmas lights in
the cans in place of candles and the light re-
flected on the metal of the cans until the shepherd glowed more than the angel above him.

With luminaries and tamales, Marla felt as
if she was having one of her childhood Christ-
mases.

The light from the luminary shepherd also
made it possible to see the other shepherds.
One shepherd was made from what looked like
an old scarecrow. The scarecrow's hat had been

replaced by a simple robe and the figure had a cane in its hand. Another shepherd was simple cardboard cut to the shape of a shepherd. And then the last shepherd was standing so still it took Marla a minute to realize who it was. Mr. Morales was standing there. He even had a real lamb in his arms.

Mrs. Hargrove walked over to stand beside Marla. "Do you like them?"

"They're beautiful."

The older woman nodded. "We wanted to make Sammy feel good."

Marla looked over at her son. He was looking from the shepherds to Les and then back again. "I think you've done that."

"Good."

Someone with a microphone climbed the church steps and led everyone in singing "Silent Night." Marla pulled the wagon to the table that had been set up for serving the cocoa. Linda helped her lift the box onto the table, then they both moved closer to the Nativity figures. Marla glanced over to where Les stood with her son. Les had to be the one who had made the tin-can shepherd. She'd seen all the cans he had in his recycle bin in the barn. Who else would have that many cans all the same size?

* * *

Les told himself that this was peace. For the first time he had to agree that the Nativity project was worth all the soup everyone had eaten for months. People gathered around the figures as though they were expecting them to spring to life right in front of them then and there. Maybe it was because Mr. Morales was standing with the plastic figures and he had let the lamb down so it could wander around. There was life mixed in with all of the lit-up plastic.

Sammy was standing beside him and Les let his hand rest on the boy's shoulder. The two teenagers who'd been arrested the other night had confessed to the deputy in Miles City that they had been harassing Sammy. He had never been a full member of the 19th Street gang. Les was glad of that. Not because he wouldn't stand beside Sammy if he had to pay the consequences for anything he had done in his young life. Les just didn't want Sammy to have seen the hard things that those two teenagers had seen.

He figured the teenagers would do some time in a juvenile facility and then face some additional probation time.

There was always a price to be paid for mistakes, Les told himself. But there was a world of mercy, too. He had to remind himself of that when he looked over at Marla.

Marla had moved closer to the Nativity figures, along with Linda. Both women looked as if they were enjoying the singing, although Linda kept edging away from the Nativity as though she had something else to do.

Before long, Linda had made her way to Les's side.

"I'll look after Sammy and Mrs. Hargrove has Becky," Linda said. "Here's your chance."

"Now?" Les had pictured a nice quiet conversation with Marla. Someplace where all his neighbors weren't gathered.

"She's planning to move after Christmas."

"So soon?"

Linda nodded.

Well, Les hadn't worked with animals in his life without learning that sometimes it was all about the timing of things. If now was the only time he had to take his chance, he meant to take it.

Marla was only vaguely aware of how the singing voices were changing around her. Linda's soprano voice had faded and a deep bass voice was growing nearer. She wasn't paying too much attention, though. The words of the Christmas carols were all she heard. They made her believe it was truly possible to have peace on earth and goodwill to men.

"Hi," someone whispered near her ear.

Marla didn't have to look to know it was Les. She frowned. The goodwill-to-men sentiment was becoming a little more difficult to maintain. Still, she hadn't had a chance to thank Les. Or to give him back those gloves of his. She pulled the gloves off her hands.

"Here." Marla gave them to him. "I've wanted to return these."

Les frowned. "But you'll need them. You don't have any gloves."

Marla curled her hands into balls and stuck them into her pockets. "They're your gloves, and I'll do just fine. Thank you."

Les was still looking at her. "What's the point of keeping your toes warm in those socks if you freeze your fingers off in the meantime?"

Marla became very still. Her hands weren't the only part of her that was turning cold. "You know about the socks?"

"Of course."

He said it as if it was such an easy thing and no betrayal at all, Marla thought. "Who else knows?"

"Well, I suppose Linda knows. Or at least, it was her idea. And if Linda knows, then…"

Marla spun around. Two of the people who she thought were closest to being her friends were the ones who had started the charity-box business. What did they do, anyway? Sit around and talk about all the things she and her children didn't have? It was humiliating.

She was going home.

Marla took only one step before she remembered the children. This was Sammy's moment. He was standing beside Linda looking at those shepherds as if they'd been made just for him. And they had. She turned in the other direction and saw Becky snuggled up beside Mrs. Hargrove. The older woman was wearing a long coat and Becky was standing inside the folds of it with just her face poking out.

She might be stomping off to go home, but her children had already found a home. Was her pride worth taking the children away from all that? Marla knew she had bad memories of charity boxes and things like that from her childhood. But, maybe, sometimes charity was just a community helping their own. Her mother had made receiving charity seem like such a shameful thing. Was it possible for her to accept charity and not make Sammy and Becky feel bad about it?

She looked around her. She had to stay in Dry Creek. This was their home. She might have to swallow her pride every day she lived here, but she would do it for her children.

Everyone was singing "Hark the Herald Angels Sing" and Les was over talking to Linda and then they were both walking toward her. Great. This was just what she needed. Marla did a couple of quick blinks so neither one of them would see that her eyes had started to tear up. There would be enough time to cry when she got back to her home. It might be a humble home and they might not have all the things other people in Dry Creek had, but they were here to stay and—

"Here," Les said as he pushed Linda forward. "She'll tell you I mean what I say. That I'm an honest guy."

Marla noticed that the singing had stopped and everyone had turned and looked at them. Of course, Les and Linda couldn't see everyone watching, because they had their backs to them.

Linda looked a little startled, but she nodded. "Les is one hundred percent solid."

"I work hard and I own my place free and clear. Tell her."

"Les, Linda—there's—" Marla tried to tell the two that everyone was listening, but they were intent on speaking.

Linda nodded again. "He takes his duties very seriously. There's even some talk of him running for sheriff if—"

"I'll never do that." Les interrupted the other woman with a frown. "Don't make promises I can't keep. You've already messed up with the socks."

"What socks?"

Linda stood there looking bewildered and Marla felt some of the tension ease within her.

"There's people—" Marla tried again.

"What do you mean, what socks?" Les's voice was rising. "That was your suggestion. Something she needed."

"He got you *socks*?" Linda asked, turning to Marla. "That was his big romantic present to show you how he felt about you?"

Marla thought surely Linda would see everyone listening to them. Maybe she did. Les still hadn't.

"Well, I didn't think the roast was enough," Les muttered, then let his voice get louder.

"And you said I couldn't go wrong if I got her something she needed."

"But socks?" Linda shook her head.

Marla was starting to smile and she felt the warmth of it right down to her toes. "They were nice socks. Ten pair and some for each of the kids, too."

"They needed socks," Les repeated as he started smiling along with Marla.

"But where's the romance in that?" Linda protested.

"He wants her to be warm?" suggested one of the people watching.

Linda shrugged. "Well, maybe that works."

Les looked up at their audience, and the thought crossed his mind that his parents had never once had a public argument about socks.

"Very, very warm," Les added as he put his arm around Marla and realized he didn't even mind all the onlookers. He was beginning to think that if the only way two people could communicate was to yell everything out in a crowd as his parents had done, it was still best to communicate. Otherwise, a man ended up giving a woman socks when she really wanted—

"I still don't know what you want for Christmas," Les whispered.

"I haven't got anything for you, either," Marla whispered back.

Then someone in the crowd yelled out, "Have they kissed and made up yet? I can't hear what they're saying."

Sometimes, Les thought, an audience could even have the right idea.

Marla saw the affection in Les's eyes as he dipped his head and gave her a kiss. She wasn't sure when someone started singing again, but she wondered if the song was something about stars. Or were the stars what she was seeing? All she could remember were the stars she'd seen that night when she snuggled up against Les's back when they were riding the horse together.

"Merry Christmas," Les lifted his head to whisper.

He didn't even give her a chance to repeat the greeting to him before he kissed her again.

Epilogue

Everyone in Dry Creek, except Marla, knew Les was going to propose. Of course, he hadn't told anyone he was going to ask Marla to marry him. The citizens of Dry Creek had known Les since he was a boy, however, and they had never seen him carry a dozen red roses down the street in Dry Creek before— and certainly not in the middle of a snow flurry. They had also never heard him stand by a woman's front door and try to serenade her with an old love song from the forties. Fortunately, it hadn't been snowing that time, but it was windy enough that shutters were slamming this way and that all over town and half the dogs were howling.

It was clear that Les hadn't wanted to be seen or heard, and that only added to the gossip. There was so much talk about Les's unusual behavior that the old men who sat around the woodstove in the hardware store started to make predictions on when Les would give up trying to impress Marla and just pop the age-old question.

Charley thought the younger man wouldn't make it through January. Charley had been a farmer all his life and he knew Les had already started his calving season. A farmer didn't get his full quota of sleep during calving season and his resistance would be down. An impatient man would just say what was on his mind and forget about dressing it up with frills.

On the other hand, Mr. Morales, who came to sit with the old men at times, said Les would most likely wait to propose on Valentine's Day, because women liked the grand romance of that kind of timing.

Once Mr. Morales had spoken, they all agreed that it must be what Les was planning. It only made sense. Les had always been practical. He lived an orderly life and he would pay attention to things like the calendar. Besides, Les himself must know he wasn't a romantic kind of a man. He could use the help of Valentine's Day to back up his proposal. What man couldn't?

The old men all nodded to each other and

decided Valentine's Day would be it. Pastor Matthew, who clerked part-time at the hardware store, even bought a couple of bottles of sparkling cider to keep in the small refrigerator behind the counter so that they could all celebrate when they heard the good news.

The men kept watch out the hardware-store window all day on Valentine's Day, but they didn't see anything unusual. Eventually Les did show up to take Marla to dinner at the café, but the two kids were with them when they left Marla's house and none of the men thought Les would be so unromantic as to propose in front of the children.

When Valentine's Day came and went without a proposal, the men were disappointed and more than a little concerned. Les might not be as flamboyant as other men when it came to courting a woman, but the men had all figured he would eventually gather enough courage to ask the big question. It was the sort of thing a man had to do if he expected to gain a wife.

There was some discussion about what they could do to help Les. Eventually, they decided it wouldn't do Les's confidence any good for him to know how worried they were. Still, they had to do something, so they went to see Mrs. Hargrove.

"He's just giving her space," Mrs. Hargrove said. She was standing beside her open door because the men had asked their question as they stood on her porch. "Young people are big on this space stuff."

"If he gives her enough space, she'll plumb leave town," Charley grumbled.

"Women didn't need space when we were young," Elmer muttered.

"Well, times are different now," Mrs. Hargrove said firmly. "Besides, Marla just became a Christian. Maybe Lester is being considerate and giving her time to adjust to the changes in her life."

The men were all silent for a moment as they looked at their boots. They wondered if Les wasn't being too considerate, but they didn't have nerve enough to say that to Mrs. Hargrove.

"That cider the pastor bought isn't going to keep forever," Charley finally muttered, and they turned to leave.

The men decided there was nothing they could do, but they did, unconsciously or not, feel a little bit of sorrow every time they talked to Les. If their conversation happened to turn a time or two in the direction of how a man needed courage in his life, they meant well by their words.

If Les understood what they were trying to tell him, he never indicated it.

By the end of March, the men in the hardware store had run out of predictions. Les had not only missed Valentine's Day, he'd also missed Lincoln's Birthday and St. Patrick's Day. The men reluctantly agreed that Les simply wasn't going to ask Marla to marry him.

When they heard Les had finally given in to Mrs. Hargrove's pleas and agreed to sing a solo in church on Palm Sunday, they decided he was turning his thoughts to other things besides romance. And they would be there to show their support. After all, not all men were called to be married. They decided they would give him some of that space Mrs. Hargrove talked about.

Les's voice rang out clearly that Sunday morning as he sang about the palms that had been laid before Jesus as He made His triumphant entry into Jerusalem. If Les smiled a little more than usual, everyone just figured it was because he was imagining what it would have been like to see Christ on that first Palm Sunday.

It wasn't until just before the closing prayer

that Pastor Matthew announced that Les had an announcement to make.

Even when Les turned and held out his hand to Marla, it took a few seconds for the old men to realize what was happening.

The pleased, pink smile on Marla's face told the whole story, though.

"I'll be," Elmer muttered. "He did it without us."

"I guess she had enough of that space," Charley whispered to Mrs. Hargrove.

Les didn't even get all his words out before the congregation was clapping away.

"You could get married right now," someone called out.

Les shook his head. "We've got it all planned."

"It'll be soon," Marla added with a smile. "And you're all invited."

The wedding was in May. Several women from the church helped Marla prepare enough sweet pork tamales to feed everyone for the reception. Marla knew her Hispanic roots were completely accepted in this small town when everyone ate their tamales with such enjoyment. She wished her aunts and uncles from Mexico could be with her, but they had sent a beautiful veil made of Mexican lace for her to wear. And Mr. Morales had become as dear to her as her own uncles. The shepherd walked her down the aisle and was the first one to shout "Hallelujah" when Les kissed her for the first time after they became husband and wife.

* * * * *

Dear Reader,

The Christmas season never ceases to move me and I like nothing better than to read, or write, a Christmas book. That's probably why my first Dry Creek novel, *An Angel for Dry Creek*, was set around the small town's Christmas pageant. I had great fun focusing on the angel in the Nativity story. Angels dazzle, after all. They sizzle. They have loud voices and great news to impart. What's not to love about an angel?

For some reason, though, shepherds aren't so readily embraced. They have no special powers. No flashing lights. No halos. They are simple working men doing the best they can for their sheep. They're usually not handsome or debonair. What they are is dependable. While their sheep are sleeping, the shepherds are guarding them. Shepherds protect their flocks; they fight off any wolves that come around. They are the quiet heroes of everyday life.

In *Shepherds Abiding in Dry Creek* I deliberately chose a hero, Les Wilkerson, who is like a shepherd. He has no swagger to him, no poetry. But you can rely on him to keep his promises and to be there when you need him. He will keep you safe.

I've known men like Les and I'm sure you have, too. It's easy to take such men for granted. If you have a shepherd hero in your life, Christmas is a good time to say a special thanks to him for his steadfastness.

Thanks for reading *Shepherds Abiding in Dry Creek*. May it add to the richness of your Christmas season.

Sincerely yours,

Janet Tronstad

QUESTIONS FOR DISCUSSION

1. Marla's husband asks for forgiveness and then dies before there is time for Marla to talk to him. Have you ever forgiven someone when there was no way you could talk to them directly about what had happened? Did you use any special techniques? How did it feel for you to forgive this person?

2. Part of the reason it was so difficult for Marla to forgive her husband was that she wondered if he thought she was inadequate as a wife. What types of things make a woman feel inadequate as a wife?

3. What are some thoughts from the Bible that define what a good wife is?

4. What are some things we can do to remind ourselves of how God sees us in all our roles?

5. Marla moved to Dry Creek so her children would have a better/safer life. She was particularly worried that her son might be getting involved in a gang. Do you think she did the best thing by moving away? Should

she have stayed and helped her son battle the temptation toward gang life? What would you do?

6. How do you think a community should respond to things like the stolen shepherd? Did the community of Dry Creek handle it in the best way? What else could they have done?

7. Part of the reason Sammy got into so much trouble was that he was keeping secrets from his mother. How should communities encourage children to seek help from adults when they are in trouble?

8. Part of Sammy's punishment was to help Mrs. Hargrove with her Sunday-school class. Is this a punishment for someone like Sammy? Why or why not?

9. Marla worried that her Hispanic heritage would not be accepted in a place like Dry Creek. Think of times when you have been the different one in the group. What did you learn from that experience? What did Marla do to share her heritage?

10. Les learned not to let his fears of becoming like his parents limit his life. What fears hold you back in your life?

Get 2 Free Books,
Plus 2 Free Gifts —
just for trying the Reader Service!

Love Inspired®

Get 2 Free Books,
Plus 2 Free Gifts—
just for trying the Reader Service!

LIS17R2

Get 2 Free Books,
Plus 2 Free Gifts—
just for trying the Reader Service!

Love Inspired HISTORICAL

Get 2 Free Books,
Plus 2 Free Gifts—
just for trying the
Reader Service!

♦HARLEQUIN®

HEARTWARMING™

Get 2 Free Books,
Plus 2 Free Gifts—
just for trying the Reader Service!